The Vast Clear Blue

Karen Winters Schwartz

The Vast Clear Blue
Red Adept Publishing, LLC
104 Bugenfield Court
Garner, NC 27529
https://RedAdeptPublishing.com/

This is a work of fiction. Names, characters, places, and incidents either are the product of the author's imagination or are used fictitiously, and any resemblance to locales, events, business establishments, or actual persons—living or dead—is entirely coincidental.

---

1.   http://StreetlightGraphics.com

To all the eccentric individuals who make up the ex-pat population of Belize, and more specifically to that frenzied stranger we met in the outback who inspired this story.

Chapter 1: If She Were a Hen

"I would have sex with that chicken," she stated.

Mark laughed. What the hell was she talking about? But then he laughed again, and she joined him, because of course she would not have sex with a chicken. She was simply putting herself in the place of the hens that they were watching through the car window—the hens that scratched and pecked at the earth of Belize. He was a handsome bird, strutting among the hens. His long golden feathers shimmered in the sun as he cocked his head this way and that, scanning the ground for some lovely morsel.

Was there any part of himself, Mark wondered from his place in the back seat of the car, that resembled this rooster? Certainly not his hair, which was a short, wild mess of fuzzy black; and never, not even when it was wet, had his hair ever glistened in the sun. He hoped his eyes were large and soulful—he did not wish them to be beady and fowl-like. But the regal air of the bird—that was something he'd like to own. Something, perhaps, she would be after if she were a hen.

He'd known Kendal a short time. Days only, and already, he understood her random utterances—or thought he did. He didn't know, as of yet, why she was here, even though he'd told her everything. He told everybody everything—if they stood there long enough, or if they shared a Belikin with him at a local bar, or if he met them on the beach or walking down the road of Hopkins. That was how he'd met Aaron, on the main road of Hopkins. It was at a local restaurant that Aaron had first introduced him to Kendal. And the two of them, Aaron and

Kendal, had taken him on as a friend and a new set of eyes as they shared with him their beloved Belize.

Now they were here, in Kendal, Belize, admiring the chickens as they waited for Aaron. He knew why she was here, in Kendal—wanting to show him the place that shared her name—but why Belize? He'd asked her, of course, but had not, as of yet, received a proper answer.

Kendal, Belize, Central America. Not coming anywhere close to the woman who shared its name. It was a ramshackle place set along the Southern Highway, its small, sad shacks near the washed-out bridge—the "temporary" wooden structure over the Sittee River forcing drivers to infiltrate the edges of this tiny Maya village. But even if, by American standards, Kendal fell short of a decent place to live, there was a certain beauty and quaintness to this community, dotted with lush plants, sprinkled with colorful fowl, and inhabited by small, happy, dark-skinned people.

He remembered the first time the poignant pleasure of Belize had struck him, hard and almost senseless. It was during the bus ride from the airport, zipping along the Hummingbird Highway as if buses defied almost every law of physics, his black plastic bag of cold Belikins chattering and sweating between his feet, one cool bottle of the beer held firmly in his hand. The bus was hot and stuffy; the steamy air blasting in from the windows did little to dispel the general odor of crowded, overheated humans—the combination of sweat and urine and beer, mingled with the occasional scent of an orange someone sliced open or a floral whiff wafting through the windows.

He'd watched with amazement as the flat countryside, scattered with brush and palmettos, began to change and thicken with greenery and then began to seethe up into soft hills. Then, quite suddenly, they were in the dense drama of the jungle-covered Maya Mountains. Astoundingly breathtaking views flashed by his window: jungle hillsides, tall fans of ferns, huge palms, yellow flowers highlighting the canopy, row after row of orange trees, one tiny village or small farm after the other. The beer—three empty bottles clanking with five remaining—now safely pulsating through his bloodstream helped to enhance the feeling of awe. And then the quick flashing glimpses of the small piles of debris, the half-finished structures, concrete blocks stretching toward the sky; rusty abandoned cars; the exaggerated hip bones of horses staked to eat the slight offerings of grass by the road; a naked, forgotten doll, its arms twisted in a broken sort of way; a white dog so thin that it almost staggered gratefully into the path of the bus.

He was slapped by the beauty and the ugliness and how the two blended into one another in a soft sigh. He tilted his head back and drew in a long cool drink of the Belikin; and when his gaze returned to the window, he saw the crushed school bus nearly reclaimed by the jungle, a pretty vine with large purple flowers snaking through the broken windows, its tires pointing skyward in a small valley. But before he could truly process it, the image was gone. His own bus rose up, and it seemed to leave the pavement. He looked forward, and they were hurtling toward the green lushness of a mountain, and he closed his eyes involuntarily, unwilling to entertain the visual of his impending death.

It was fitting that it should end this way—a fiery crash in the jungle—and how many years would it take for someone to view what remained and not feel some sort of sadness? How many years until all that was left was a tangle of green? But when he was forced to reopen his eyes, the bus was skittering around a curve then cruising effortlessly up another mountain, and he put his head down and vomited neatly into his bag of beer. He set the bag back between his feet and felt the warmth mingling with the cold as it seeped through the plastic and settled around his sandals.

He had, of course, survived the bus ride. His intention had been to settle in Placencia, remembering it as a laid-back, sleepy fishing village with cute, colorful buildings and beautiful beaches. The memories were soft and quixotic. Cathy stretched out on the beach—her long, dark hair splayed upon the sand, tiny beads of sweat between her breasts—pouring cold beer onto her stomach, and the salty, bitter sensation of sucking it from her navel. The night they'd skinny-dipped—the wet sea slipping between their legs, the unseen creatures slithering in the dark waters, freaking each other out—fleeing the sea and running naked and screaming across the sand back to their cabana, their wet slimy bodies coming together with frenzied glee, laughing hysterically in each other's arms. Then the overpowering need to be in her—pushing her to the bed, her body dotted with tiny pieces of seaweed, a fine dusting of sand between her thighs, her arms reaching out and pulling him down. It had been the most intense orgasm he'd ever had.

His best sex, already behind him?

Author Note: "Everybody here has a story!" our friend, Chuck, exclaimed when he was visiting Paul and me in Belize. Strange and beautiful, southern Belize and the people who call it home excite endless stories that are unbelievable, funny, and poignant. The inspiration for The Vast Clear Blue occurred when Paul, Chuck, and I were bouncing along the roads of Central America and had a two-minute conversation with a frenetic stranger in a sedan. He was a slightly crazed American who'd flagged us down while attempting to drive across a fast-flowing river in search of a waterfall. Although I never caught his name, he told us more in those two minutes than I would have thought possible. He really got the three of us going: "What is up with that dude?" "What the heck is his story?" "He looks totally crushed." "He's not crushed—he's just wacked!" We spent the car ride home making up all sorts of possible scenarios. The Vast Clear Blue is my love song to this quirky, unique little country. I hope it touches you like Belize has touched me. Thanks for reading! (I wonder if my friend in the sedan ever found his waterfall?)

Chapter 2: Upside-Down Bananas

But Mark never made it back to Placencia. When the bus stopped for a quick rest in Dangriga, he'd thankfully staggered from it, relished the stillness of the earth and the sound of the sea. Then he just simply did not reboard. Hours later, he was laughing, drinking coconut rum, and smoking weed with some locals on the beach. There was a vague memory of a crazy ride in the back of a pickup and then the more painful memory of waking up spooning his luggage, his face nestled into the coarse white sand, his shoulder already burned in the weak morning sun.

"Hey! Man!" he'd called while freeing grains of sand from his ear canal. "Where am I?"

The warm laughter from the tall, dark man who strolled toward his fishing boat reached his ears over the gentle pulse of the waves. "Hopkins, mon. You're in Hopkins."

And that's where he'd settled—in the strange and beautiful Garifuna village, abundant with warm laughter and as welcoming as a soft bed.

He and Kendal both looked up from the chickens at the same time to see Aaron walking toward them from some distance. Even from this significant span, they could see that he had a large white bag flung over his back and that he was bouncing with enthusiasm.

"What's he got?"

"He's found it," Kendal said dryly. "The Holy Grail of Belize."

"Huh?"

She didn't answer him, and as Aaron grew closer, he said, "I hope it's not full of dead chickens," which made her laugh. She and Aaron both tended toward vegetarianism, eating fish as their only occasional meat—something he was considering for himself, but damn, he loved a good steak.

"You're not going to believe it!" Aaron called as soon as his voice could be heard. "You won't fucking Belize it!" He laughed with glee as he reached the battered Chevy Tracker and opened its rear door. He threw the bag into the back space none too gently, and the thudding sound precluded the possibility of dead chickens. "Mark! You're gonna love this!"

"Coconuts?" he asked.

"Are you fucking kidding me? Coconuts? Why the fuck would I pay for coconuts? The fuckers are everywhere!"

Mark did a mental count: three "fucks" in three seconds, three different variations. Aaron's ability to seamlessly use that particular expletive was impressive.

"Banana trees!" Aaron continued. "Twelve of them!" He pushed a strand of long dirty-blond hair that had escaped from his ponytail out of his eyes and left a dirty smudge across his forehead.

Mark considered the bag skeptically. "Twelve banana trees?"

"Yes! Listen! Listen!" Aaron said as he shut the back door and made his way to the driver's side. "This is just crazy!" He opened the door, got in, and slammed it with flair. He flashed a smile Kendal's way. Mark contemplated that flash of a smile and the way Kendal's eyes brightened as she met Aaron's look; then Aaron turned toward Mark as he said, "So I say to the little guy, 'I want some banana trees to plant. Some kind that will grow near the ocean.' And he takes me to this clump of these really tall and lush banana trees and tells me that this is the kind I want. And I look at them and think, 'Wow! These are really nice, but they're big and lush.' There were some little ones, but I'm still thinking they're gonna cost a bundle to dig up and move. So I ask him,

'How much?' And he thinks a moment, and I'm expecting to have to barter with him, and then he says, 'Fifty cents?' Like, twenty-five cents in US, and I'm fucking floored. 'Well... okay. I'll take twelve,' I say, and I'm trying to calculate if they're all gonna fit in the car and if it would hurt them if they stuck out of the back. But before I know it, he has this machete, and he's chopping the hell out of these trees, banana leaves flying everywhere, and he hands me—" Aaron stopped talking, took a breath, and jumped out of the car. He ran around to the back again and opened up the rear door. He pulled a sandy stump out of the sack and threw it at Mark. Mark caught it, just barely, as Aaron said, "And this is what I got! A dozen of them!"

Mark studied the fat, decapitated trunk, a few scant roots clinging to its bottom, and couldn't imagine that the thing would live.

"He said you just stick it in the ground, and in nine months, I'm gonna have bananas!" Aaron slammed the door again and made his way back to the front of the car.

"Who knew... bananas and babies... the same gestational period," Kendal stated, not quite loud enough for Aaron to hear, but her statement set Mark to laughing.

"Do you fucking believe that?" asked Aaron as he reentered the car.

Mark was still laughing when he said, "No. I don't think I do."

"You wait! You just fucking wait! I don't think I'm even gonna give you any." But he was laughing too as he cranked the engine to life and popped it into drive. The car leapt forward and then stalled with a groan. Aaron, undaunted, repeated the process, and within moments, they were back over the wooden bridge and sailing back toward Hopkins.

Kendal leaned back and placed her bare feet on the dash and said, "Isn't it odd that bananas hang upside down from banana trees?" Before Mark had much of a chance to think about this, she asked Aaron, "And where exactly are you going to plant your babies?"

Aaron pounded the steering wheel with his fingers and bobbed his head to music, which must have been blasting through his head, as the radio hadn't worked since Mark had known him. "All around the yard. It'll be a fucking botanical garden!"

"Yard?" Kendal asked, but the music must have been too loud for Aaron to hear.

Mark thought about Aaron's yard, or lack of one, as he rented nothing more than a wooden shack—an afterthought of a structure tacked onto the owner's main house. Even the main house was a poorly thrown-together concrete block, nailed-on metal roof, square openings for windows, and tattered flowered sheets as drapes. Each window sported a different floral design, which fluttered in and out of the wooden louvered windows in the sea breeze. There really wasn't a yard, and what little bit of land that accompanied the house was cluttered with old tires, bed springs, concrete blocks, broken toys, and torn fishing nets. Jonathan and Theresa were Aaron's landlords, and along with the two of them, the place was inhabited by innumerable children, dogs, cats, transitory relatives, and, of course, chickens. Mark had made it his mission to get to know each one of the children, but every time he thought he had it all figured out, suddenly, there would be another one. "What is your name? Do you live here?" he'd ask the sweet little girl grinning at him or the tiny little boy whose hands didn't ever leave his crotch, and the answers were always vague.

Not that his place was much better—only a small room above one of the guest houses of a small inn and local restaurant, with an outdoor shower and toilet on the beach that he shared with the restaurant patrons and other hotel guests. But he had a nice view of the Caribbean Sea, and it wasn't a big deal for him to piss out his window in the middle of the night rather than stagger down the stairs to the toilet. He was hardly there except to sleep, and even that wasn't every night. Yes, it was okay—suited his needs and his mood for now. And it was cheap—dirt cheap.

Before long, they were turning off the main road and bumping down the four long, straight miles of mystery that led to the coast and into Hopkins. It had been dry the last few days, so the dust was particularly bad and flew around the car. They quickly caught up to a truck that was sending plumes of dust their way, decreasing visibility. Even Aaron was not quick enough to avoid the impressive potholes, causing Kendal to perch up on the car seat like a bird, absorbing the trauma with her feet and legs. An act that Mark highly endorsed—anything and everything should be done to protect that fine ass.

Once in town, where the road improved and was even paved in some places, Aaron turned Mark's way and asked, "Want me to drop you home?"

"Nah. I'll help you bury those things." It wasn't as if he had anything else to do. And it would take some doing—cleaning up the property enough to make room for the possibility of bananas.

Author Note: Way back in 2002, I fell in love with Belize, I think before my feet ever touched its soil. You could say I fell in love at first breath. The heat, the humidity, the sunshine, the wobbly metal steps I had to negotiate as I stepped off the plane—all of it was magic and made all the sweeter because of the diversity and warmth of its people. Other than perhaps Italy, I've never felt so welcome in a foreign country. And there was one extremely important bonus: all the signs were in English! What's not to love? We bought property during that very first visit. This story is set back in those early honeymoon years of Belize. Today, many of the establishments, the state of roads and bridges, the types of cellular devices, and so on have changed or no longer exist. But that air, those people, the heat, and the signs in English remain the same!

Chapter 3: Cool Spots and Belikins

Kendal left the men to play with their bananas, as she had no interest in that sort of thing. The sun was just dipping toward the west, and it was still slicing through the air with waves of heat, limiting the foot traffic on the road and urging her toward the nearest cool spot. She turned back toward the center of town, hoping King Kassava's had reopened for the afternoon.

As she grew closer, she could see the group of young Garifuna men hanging by the bus stop. There was almost always a group that hung in front of the little grocery store across from Kassava's, but the group shifted and varied in number and members—sometimes loud and boisterous, other times quiet and respectful.

Today—with the sun beating down on her, her blond hair frizzing up from her moist scalp, her dirty bare feet attached to her long, naked legs, the small tattoo of the lizard creeping up her calf, her light T-shirt fraying over her baggy cargo shorts—it all must have been too much to bear, because the group erupted in whistles and catcalls and soft gestures of welcome.

"Kendal, Kendal, light my fire," one young man sang out in his rich Garifuna accent.

She laughed. "Settle down, boys!" she called as she turned the corner and made her way into the cool shade of the bar's outdoor seating. When she sat down, a couple of the older, bolder men broke away from the group and strolled across the street to lean against the makeshift bar, where they could be closer to any opportunity that might arise.

"Good day," Frank, the owner, called to her. Frank was probably in his early fifties, but it was hard to be sure. His dark face was heavily creased from years in the sun, but his movements and his spirit were those of a younger man.

She returned his toothy grin with her own crooked smile.

"Good day, Frank. Got a cold Belikin somewhere back there?"

"For you, lady, I got plenty." He laughed with a tiny suggestive shift of his hips. The men at the bar laughed with him and nodded in good-hearted approval.

She laughed, too, because it was easier just to go along with it. But really, could it ever just stop? Castration: it was a simple procedure—a slice, a squeeze, a snip, and a staple. She'd done it on rats in college. It had taken only moments, an almost bloodless procedure. She narrowed her eyes at the men at the bar. Almost bloodless.

It wasn't like she was God's gift to men or anything. Her blue eyes were too big and too far apart, her chin too long; her hair was a sad white woman's attempt at dreadlocks—the fuzzy clumps of twisted hair mixed with various colored threads and the occasional strand of seaweed or other beach debris. Today, the locks were pulled up off her neck in a weak, unbecoming mass.

It was the body they must be after—long and thin, but larger in all the right places. Her body was so different from those of the Garifuna women, who tended to be short and soft and plump. The Garifuna men, unlike their women, tended to be tall and lean and hard. Perhaps it was just the novelty—tall and pale and soft where it counted—that they wanted to explore.

Frank brought her the Belikin, and she ignored the men's furtive glances, turning her attention to the cold wetness and to the relief from the heat. She passed the dewy bottle across her sweaty forehead and rested it momentarily in the cleavage of her chest before actually bringing the bottle to her lips. She sighed and pulled her feet onto the other chair at the table. After a couple minutes, she pulled her paperback from her small, colorful knapsack and began to read. A few more minutes passed by as she gently turned the pages. Lost now in the story, she scarcely noticed the men as they drifted away.

Author Note: Anyone who has ever been to Belize knows what a Belikin is. Like Chianti is to Italy, Belikin beer is to Belize. For a very long time, it was virtually the only beer you could buy in Belize. Sir Barry Manfield Bowen made sure of that! As the story goes, after he bought the bottling company from his father in 1978, Bowen, a prominent leader of the People's United Party, went on to ensure that taxes on imported beer skyrocketed, and in no time at all, Belikin was the national drink. When a competitor, Charger, surfaced in the early '70s, rumor had it that Sir Bowen started buying up the empty returnable glass Charger bottles. This forced Charger to spend huge sums to import new glass bottles, effectively causing them to fail. Sir Bowen died at the age of 64 as one of Belize's wealthiest entrepreneurs when he crashed his private plane, but his beer lives on. Served in all the local cool spots, the extra-thick glass of the bottles teases you; just when you think you've only consumed half the bottle, it's suddenly empty. Guess it's time to order round two!

Chapter 4: Avocados, Papaya, and Gonads

"Kendal, there you are."

She looked up from her book, beyond her now-empty beer bottle, to Aaron's hips and then lingered there before making her way to his eyes. She was surprised to find that it was now dark and that she'd been reading from the dim lights of Kassava's. "So, we got all the trees planted! It's going to be just incredible. I was thinking I might get some papaya plants too."

Kendal removed her feet from the other chair and sat up a bit. She looked out into the dark street. These were the short days of winter, and the sun always dropped fast and hard in Belize.

"You know, they're just these funny treelike things. The fruit hangs under the leaves like long, green, gigantic gonads."

"Jolly Green Giant gonads," she added.

He pointed his cigarette at her, and they laughed. "That's right! I wonder if I could just start them from seeds. Avocados, I wonder how the fuck they grow."

She laughed again and dropped her eyes back toward his crotch, as it was an easier place for her eyes to be. This view always reminded her of the first time she'd met Aaron, right here in this place; and he'd been standing over her just as he was today and talking nonsense—just as he was today.

Her eyes could not help but linger there, that very first meeting, with him standing and her sitting down. It was a natural resting spot—a diversion from the inability to follow his words, which flitted about the room along with his cigarette ashes as he punctuated his speech with his fluttering hands. She'd studied the white stitched words of his boxers, *Calvin Klein*, that peeked above his precariously hung jeans—the possibilities licking gently at her brain. She had wanted, just as she did now, to reach out and free those jeans from his fine, thin hips and see what magic rested there.

It had been hard, back then, to follow his fast words in his beautiful South African accent. What had he been going on about that first meeting? Oh, yes, his family and how he'd come to be here. Not nonsense after all. The end of apartheid in South Africa and the change in labor laws had effectively forced his family to leave the country. Something about the inability to hire ninety percent blacks, which led to the closing of the small family-run business. His family had left South Africa in search of work, bopping around countries for a while, and one of those countries had been Belize. It hadn't worked out for his parents and his sister, but Aaron, who was twenty-seven at the time, had stayed. Now, almost two years later, he was a man who'd found his country.

"Hey." She reached up and tugged gently on his jeans. "Do you think you could sit?"

"Oh." He looked sheepish. "Sorry." He sat across from her and took in the other patrons. "Hey. Another beer?" he asked.

She shook her head, and he was up again and at the bar to get one of his own. She laughed. His constant movement amused her.

The place was filling up with the Friday-night crowd—a mixture of locals and tourists and expats like themselves. Frank turned the music up, and the place became slightly chaotic. Kendal fingered her book lovingly, closed her eyes, and took a deep breath. When she opened them, Aaron was back and standing over her again.

"Do you want to order dinner?" he asked.

Kendal shrugged, unwilling to commit. "Where's Mark?"

"Last I saw him, he was strolling down the beach with Melvin and a bag of beer."

Kendal made a face and pushed the chair with her foot—a gentle reminder.

"Sorry!" said Aaron as he sat down. "You're not hungry yet? Don't want to eat here? Don't want to eat with me? Want to go somewhere else?"

"No. Yes, not here. I want to eat with you." She laughed. "And... yes. Later."

Aaron sighed happily and leaned back to settle in with his beer. She watched him drink, studied his Adam's apple as he swallowed, admired the way his neck went into his shoulders and the shiny flop of his long ponytail that fell across his right shoulder and onto his arm. She would kill for such lovely hair. She'd never made love with someone sporting hair such as Aaron's. That first time, as he bent over her naked body, she felt—felt it now with just the thought—the sweep of sexual energy that pulsed through her body as his hair fell across her face, her chest, her bare arms. It was no wonder that men liked long, flowing hair on their women.

It had taken a while for them to fall into bed—well, not bed exactly, as it had been on the beach, on a warm fall night, with the moon just rising and the waves crashing with a rare intensity. They'd not been so foolish as to try it in the surf; unlike in the movies, she knew that water, sex, and sand were a recipe for disaster. It had been up from the surf, on a little sandy knoll protected by sea grapes and up a ways from Hopkins and up even farther from her home. It was a risky thing to do—make love with this sort of man, with silky blond hair and a face that could make your breath catch in your throat when he laughed. It was easy to sleep with men who reminded you of driftwood or your dog's best shoe, but it was hard to lie with a man that could take just too much away. And that was exactly what he'd done—taken too much away, so that now she felt less than she was when he wasn't around. If she thought too much about this, then the air she drew in was something other than air and her chest would squeeze into itself, inviting the predictable panic that was anything but dull.

Dullness was what she longed for, what she sought, and it was the gift that Belize gave to her. So she stopped thinking about what she had allowed him to take. She watched him set the bottle down, saw the smile on his face when he looked her way, and closed her mind to anything close to panic.

"Where do you want to eat?" he asked.

"Iris's? When you're done with your beer. Then I can get takeout too."

He nodded slowly. "Sounds great. I think they brought in some grouper today." He smiled. "If it were nine months from now, I could sell ol' Iris some of my bananas."

"And jolly green gonads."

He laughed. "That's right! She would love that."

Author Note: Fun Fruit Facts: Avocados were once called alligator pears.
Papaya is a large berry and can weigh as much as twenty pounds.
Even though they have seeds, gonads are not actually fruit!

Chapter 5: What Can Really Break Your Heart

Aaron finished his beer, and they walked through the south end of the village. Small wooden-and-concrete homes lined each side of the street. Huge mangrove trees and palms, banana and cashew trees, rainbows of flowering bougainvillea, and spiky yucca grew among the buildings. Hand-painted signs hung from some of the homes: Bikes For Rent, Native Art, Internet, Snorkeling, Fishing Trips, Rooms For Rent. Small, open, or fully walled structures were added to other homes, a Coke or Belikin sign hanging out front—breakfast, lunch, dinner served. To their left, immediately behind the buildings, was the Caribbean Sea. To their right were several layers of homes and then the flat sweeping beauty of marshland. And then, farther yet, were the Maya Mountains.

The small street was crowded with men and women and children and bikes and dogs. It took a long time to walk to Iris's, as Kendal and Aaron knew most of the village, and it was necessary to say goodnight to everyone. And it was difficult to stop Aaron from talking once he'd started, so that by the time they reached the small blue building, Kendal was hungry, and Aaron claimed to be near death from starvation.

It was after they'd placed their orders for fish, and Aaron was gently sipping on his beer and Kendal was sucking on her orange Fanta, that the door squeaked open and banged shut from the entry of Mark and Melvin. It was quite obvious that Mark was drunk—very drunk. He leaned on Melvin's tall, dark body in a good-natured but necessary way as they made their way to the table. Melvin helped Mark onto a chair and rolled his dark eyes their way and laughed. "Our boy's feeling his Belikins," he said in his faint Garifuna accent. "That's for fucking sure."

"Food!" Mark banged the table. "I need food! Beer! I need beer!"

"Hey, pretty lady," Melvin called toward the kitchen. "Two dinners for our stomachs."

Iris stepped from the kitchen, wiping her hands on the apron that protected the faded floral print of her skirts, and answered Melvin in Garifuna. Her dark, round face was slick with the heat and the oils of cooking, her hair pulled back and covered by a thin net. They bantered and laughed in their own language for a few minutes. Iris was still laughing as she disappeared for a moment, returning with two more Belikins. She'd adorned the lips of the bottles with a thin, folded paper napkin. "You sure you want one, baby?" she asked Mark before she set the beer down.

"Fucking A, I want a beer. I'm thirsty as 'ell."

Iris laughed and shook her head before heading back to the kitchen to start on the meals.

It was difficult to have a normal conversation as they waited for their meal. Mark was boisterous and self-absorbed in his drunken misery. When no one chose to join his verbal lamenting, to Kendal's horror, he began to croon in a pleasant but unnecessarily loud voice. Before he reached the chorus of "Only Love Can Break Your Heart," Aaron and Melvin had joined in. Kendal swore she could hear Iris singing along in the kitchen, and she was forced to place her forehead against the table. Even as they almost screamed the chorus, she could hear and smell the preparation of the fish, the hiss of the oil and the sweet, spicy odor of freshness.

Kendal, with her head still down, could see the beautiful fish swimming in the sea, just hours before. She saw its slick, spotted marbled body, its comically large mouth—laughing while frowning—having no notion of its impending death or the contribution it would make to their empty stomachs. She imagined its fins coming out with delight as it turned in midswim; its round fish eyes had spotted it—the tempting morsel floating just ahead—for the fish was hungry too. It was horrible and honorable and really the best way to die—so that other living things could survive. And this was the sort of thing, if you thought about it too much, that could really break your heart.

Author Note: Reread and remember the last two lines of this chapter. That's all I have to say in this particular author note.

Chapter 6: He Loves Me, He Loves Me Not

The three of them helped Mark home. He was staying above the Yugadah, a nice little restaurant on the main drag of Hopkins, just steps from the sea. Although the room was small and up a flight of precarious stairs, it was undeniably nicer than Aaron's. It was more than just a square place to sleep. Its two glass-louvered windows were large, one facing the sea, allowing an almost-constant breeze to cleanse the heavy air. The concrete walls were painted a fresh bright yellow; the mattress was younger than Mark, which meant something in Belize, and the large planked floors were infiltrated with minimal mildew. It was Aaron who had found the place for the new friend he'd met while cruising the streets of Hopkins a week ago. Kendal had looked down the street and seen Aaron standing uncharacteristically still and silent in the middle of the road, forcing the cars to maneuver around the potholes and the two men, a slight cock to his head as he listened.

It was later that same night, at King Kassava's, that Kendal had first looked up from her Friday-afternoon novel to see Aaron approach with Mark in tow. Mark was relatively short and slightly older than Aaron, his short dark hair as frenzied as his expression. A tragic appeal seeped off his handsome face along with a vulnerability that set her nurturing instincts aflutter. And then there was the way he looked at her and laughed at the things that escaped from her mouth—a true appreciation of the absurd that no one had ever come close to. Mark was a welcome and a fun distraction from the two of them—a relief—not from boredom but from the lack of boredom that seemed to punctuate her relationship with Aaron. The warm pleasure she felt as Mark poured himself and his heart out to the two of them in King Kassava's was so different than that very first time she'd set her eyes on Aaron.

Now, she watched as Aaron and Melvin pushed and lifted and cussed their way up the outside stairs to Mark's room. Finally reaching the top, they kicked open the door and plopped him rudely onto the mattress, leaving one leg twisted at an odd angle and the other dangling off the bed. Kendal, who had followed the men up, shook her head when they made their way loudly down the stairs, their verbal complaints unkind and unnecessary. She set her carryout dinner down and gently rearranged the body so that Mark at least appeared more presentable. She pulled up his old, threadbare sheet until it just tickled his chin, picked up her food, and shut the door softly. She joined the others on the beach.

Melvin lit a fat joint, and Kendal watched as the smoke twisted and disappeared into the fabulous display of stars. It was a beautiful night. The humidity had dropped with the temperature, and the warm tropical air sighed around them. The sea was almost calm so that the soft sound of waves mingled with the shrill singing of the peepers and the bizarre chorus of insects. Melvin passed the joint Aaron's way. It was almost in his possession when the peacefulness of the night was interrupted by the ungainly noise of Mark's rapid descent from his stairs. Once he reached the bottom step, he was apparently spent, for when they all turned toward the noise, he was splayed across the sand—a goofy smile just visible in the light from the street as his face turned their way. He struggled briefly to right himself then fell back into the sand and relaxed into laughter.

"Jesus Christ!" said Aaron with a laugh. "I'm not fucking carrying him back up those stairs."

"We can't just leave him there," said Kendal.

"Why the fuck not?"

"That white boy is staying right where he is," laughed Melvin. "Not like a croc is gonna get him."

"Hey. That's an idea." Aaron pointed his finger at Melvin then plucked the joint from his still-extended hand. "If we drag him closer to the river, he'd be a nice snack." Aaron brought the joint to his lips and began to amble down the beach, his long legs stretching out before him, the *flip-flop* of his sandals monopolizing the night. Melvin fell in beside him, and Kendal stood, conflicted.

"Guys. Really, we shouldn't just leave him," she offered weakly. They didn't hesitate or return a word. She knew it was useless. Aaron was not one to change his mind about anything. And Melvin... Well, he couldn't care less. She waved a hand at them in dismissal. "Whatever." And turned back toward Mark.

He grinned up at her as she drew near. "My savior," he slurred.

She offered him a hand, and he managed a wobbly stand. "Don't you want to go to sleep?"

"I want to go to the beach." And he was off and shuffling through the sand, slipping as he got within ten feet of the surf, letting gravity take over so that he started on his knees and worked his way to his ass. He grinned back at her and patted the sand. "Come. Sit by me."

She laughed with a sigh and joined him. For a while, the only sound was the softness of their breath and the eternal shift of the seas. It was nice, this relative silence, but it was ephemeral and rudely broken by Mark's words. "I love you, Kendal."

She closed her eyes to the dark churning sea. "No, you don't."

"I do." Then he was on her, kissing her with his drunkenness. She set her lips and waited. He pulled away. Her gaze returned to the sea. "You're messing with me." His words were mild accusations.

"You're messing with yourself," she stated. She could feel, as she stared out onto the water, his eyes on her with disbelief, and then the shift and the welcome release of his laughter.

"I'm messing with myself!" he howled with glee. He fell back onto the sand. "Mess, mess, messing myself!" He writhed about in his pleasure for a moment before he grew quiet.

She waited, and it wasn't long before his breathing had changed and turned into the soft snore of sleep. She made her way back toward the road and up the stairs to his room. She removed the sheet and his thin pillow from his bed. He didn't stir as she lifted his head onto the pillow and tucked the sheet around his body. Her fingers lingered in the roughness of his hair before they stretched into a fan, and she used his skull for leverage as she stood. "You're a jerk," she whispered, and then she turned and headed toward home.

Author Note: One thing I really enjoy—and I'm told I do well—is to write from a man's point of view. All my early years and young adult years, my besties were boys and later men. Primarily because I generally didn't like to do what girls did back in the early '60s. Perhaps it's easier with the current generation to be a girl and get down and dirty with the Earth, but back then, "girly" things just didn't cut it for me. Maybe that's one reason that I really fell in love with Kendal. But while I cannot imagine her ever playing with baby dolls, when it comes right down to it, Kendal is a woman, and only a woman's nurturing instincts would make it impossible to walk away without tucking Mark in!

Chapter 7: Death: The Ultimate Solution to Life

He woke as if he was falling or a large fish was taking him down. Once he was fully conscious, he was not floating on an unforgiving sea but safe and secure in his leather chair that looked out over the ocean. But the ocean was gone, and his world was dark, and where exactly were his feet? Even if he'd somehow survived all his years with the sea, he'd been taken down by time, and now there was no telling what time it was or how he was to go on from this spot of elderly suspension. He managed to locate his feet, which were tangled in the light blanket his wife had tucked around him in the morning. But surely he must have moved at some point during the day, as it was obvious as his mind began to clear that the sun had set while he was sleeping and it was now well into night.

It took some maneuvering, but he made his way to the bathroom and sighed from one of the only two real pleasures his old body could still withstand—pissing and eating. It had come down to that. Thank God he still had his teeth and his penis.

When he was done, he fumbled for the light and was shocked for the thousandth time by the old man in the mirror. Even the fire in his blue eyes was snuffed out. Isn't that how all the descriptions of the elderly went? *His face was old, but the fire of life still burned in his eyes... the deep cracks of time telling a story upon his face...* Well, it was bullshit, all bullshit! And then he began to laugh, because really, he wasn't that bitter old man. Old. But not bitter. He caught a glimpse of his eyes as he turned away from the mirror, and there it was—a spark of fire.

He made his way back through the dark house and into the kitchen. The light as he opened the fridge set his eyes to blinking as he studied its contents. He frowned. He glanced at the time, which glowed green over the stove. Almost seven. Really, his wife should be home by now. Well, he'd eat without her. It's not like he couldn't fend for himself. But a second, more thorough search of the fridge offered nothing that appealed to him. His knobby fingers claimed a beer, and he shut the refrigerator door. After removing a bag of chips from the cabinet, he flipped on the side-table light and settled painfully back into his chair, only to realize he'd forgotten to open his beer. He sighed at the distance between himself and the opener on its hook by the refrigerator. He struggled momentarily with the twist-off cap and then leaned back in frustration. Damn woman! Where was she?

"Charlie, why are you eating that junk? I told you I'd bring dinner home." He hadn't even heard her come in. Had he said those words? He grinned up at her, and she leaned down and kissed his lips. Her fingers lingered on his cheek. "I'm sorry I'm late," she said. She made a face. "I was detained by the needy."

"Mark?" he asked.

She nodded with a sigh. She opened his beer with a quick turn of her wrist and went to the kitchen to warm his food in the microwave.

"Iris's grouper." She smiled as she placed it on his lap. She sat down in her chair and placed her feet on the stool.

Charlie admired the beautiful filet and the large mound of beans and rice as he picked up his fork. Would he ever catch a grouper of his own again? He brought a sliver of meat to his mouth and closed his eyes to the sensation on his tongue.

"He kissed me." He opened his eyes and shot a look her way. She laughed. "Says he loves me."

"He probably does."

She shook her head. "No, just lust."

Oh, lust. What he wouldn't give to feel that again. And what lust this woman could elicit, like nothing any woman had done for him before—not his early sexual endeavors, not his first wife, nor his numerous affairs. No woman could come close to Kendal. Forget all the grouper in the sea; just let him have one more chance at lust.

His decline had been a rapid thing—first the diagnosis of diabetes, four years ago. Something he should have known was coming, type 2 diabetes being sprinkled throughout both sides of his family. But still, he'd been in denial—stubbornly ignored his symptoms—the diagnosis coming well into the disease. Maybe he'd failed to take care of himself, at least at the beginning. But then came that first stroke, shocking him into obedience. All those lectures from the doctors finally hitting home. By then, perhaps it was too late—the damage already done. Because it wasn't long before the second stroke and then the complication of severe ischemic heart disease, choking away his energy, turning him into an old man before sixty-five years of life had passed. And really, there was no one to blame other than himself and his poor genes mixed with a cavalier attitude.

They'd gone to Miami after the first stroke—caught a hopper from Dangriga, spent a day at the hospital in Belize, and then on to Miami. He hadn't bothered to leave Hopkins after his second stroke but let Nurse Ruth tend to him. Nurse Ruth, a Belizean who'd worked years in the States, ran her own clinic in the village. She was Hopkins's best source of medical care. So much better than Miami. Miami had been a needless nightmare.

All the chrome and shiny glass, neat nurses speaking Spanish, young, confident doctors—none of them could do a thing other than pump him full of needles and drugs. His daughters had flounced into his hospital room all panicky, angry, and self-righteous, as if Belize had caused his stroke—or better yet, Kendal. And Kendal, poor Kendal. Looking worse than he must have looked—worse than he'd ever seen her look—he could see her decompensate before his very eyes.

His older daughter, Claire, in a slick tan linen suit, a splash of colored silk around her neck, fluffed up his pillow in a no-nonsense sort of way. "You see, Dad, this is the sort of thing that can happen," she said, her eyes flicking to Kendal. "You need to take better care of yourself." Julie was at the foot of his bed, dressed a little less Lord and Taylor, biting at her long lacquered nails and tapping her incredibly impractical shoes against the polished linoleum of his hospital room. She patted at his legs, tucked in his sheets. He turned his head, with effort, in search of Kendal. His eyes found her sitting on the vinyl chair, her legs pulled up to her chest, her baggy hiking pants dirty at the cuffs. She must have dropped her sandals somewhere in the room, because her toes curled over the edge of the chair as if she were holding on. "Living the way you do," his daughter continued. "Where you live. It's no wonder."

Kendal was suddenly up and moving toward the door. He'd tried to call her name, but all that came out was a coarse croak, his voice temporarily lost to him, his eyes tracking her swaying movement until she'd disappeared.

Claire and Julie gave her a quick glance of dismissal before returning all their attention to him. "Maybe now you'll be coming home to Miami, where you belong."

So he'd absorbed the brunt of his daughters' anger and their anxiety. Forced himself to recover quickly, picked up a stupidly huge bag of medication, gathered up what was left of his wife, and they'd both gotten the hell out of Miami.

It was unlikely that his daughters would ever forgive him for leaving after their mother's death, even though they were grown with families of their own and called him once a month at best. But when he cashed in some of his stock a few months after their mother had died and bought the sailboat, you would have thought he'd decided to start a nudist colony in the backyard of his home. Then he sold the home in Miami, kissed his grandbabies goodbye, hugged his daughters, and took off alone on his boat. He tacked his way around the tip of Florida, negotiated Cuba, hung out in Mexico for a while, and then worked his way south through the tricky reefs of Belize. It was fifteen years ago when he first caught sight of Hopkins.

He was sailing inside the barrier reef and noticed the little buildings clustered near the middle of the bay south of Dangriga. He brought his binoculars to his eyes and studied the lovely white beach—the light-blue, orange, yellow, pink, and gray menagerie of structures mixed in with the shade of palms—and thought he might just have to check this place out. The waters were way too shallow for the draft of his boat, but his maps told him that just a bit farther south was the mouth of the Sittee River. If he could just move his boat up the river, it should get him close. The brown waters of the river were in no great hurry to meet the sea, and he traveled almost effortlessly up the river. A few lazy crocodiles slid silently into the waters as his boat drew near. Snowy egrets studied the boat with quiet concentration, while the great blue herons crackled their complaint, raising their impressive bodies into the sky.

It was less than two miles upriver where he discovered the new home for his boat, a small marina offering the perfect protection. It was just a few miles' walk down dusty dirt roads back to Hopkins, and once he stepped onto the main road of the village, he fell in love. He fell in love with the Garifuna smiles, the dilapidated little buildings they called home, the mangos dropping from the trees onto the road, the debris-covered beaches, the scattering of chickens and dogs, the barefoot children that played in the surf, the laziness and underlying excitement for life.

Initially, he lived on the boat, hoofing it into town when he couldn't catch a ride. It didn't take long for the contrast of the isolation of the river and the intimacy of the village to become too much, so he chose intimacy and moved into the village. And this village, which he loved, opened its heart to him, and he became a part of the thing—part of this town and the assortment of Garifuna natives, Creoles, red-eyed

Rastafarians, Chinese grocery store owners, Maya and Guatemalan workers, retired expats, fortune-seeking and displaced foreigners, transient hikers and tourists.

Then there was the day, ten years ago, when he walked out of the grocery store only to see the young girl—hoisting a backpack half her size, crazy tufts of early blond dreadlocks sprouting from her head—plodding into the village, and he fell in love all over again. Loving this woman, half his age, and ultimately marrying her... it was unlikely his daughters would ever forgive him for that one either.

He swallowed the rice and beans he'd been chewing and turned to her. His face rose into a smile as he said, "Maybe you should consider a little mercy sex for poor ol' Mark."

"No," she said solemnly. "Mark's too broken. I don't need broken."

"Maybe you could fix him." He took a bite of fish. He grimaced in pain and brought his fingers into his mouth.

"Maybe. But not with sex."

It took some doing, but he finally located the offending bone and pulled it from his mouth. When he'd recovered, he turned to her and studied her a moment. He knew if sex was an option with Mark, she would not be telling him this, or that by telling him this, sex was now not an option.

"So, how's Aaron?" It was a cruel thing to ask—if it was true—and he almost regretted it.

There was a beat of silence, then: "Thrilled about his new banana trees. Mark helped him plant these nubs all over Jonathan's little yard. In nine months, he'll have bananas." She smiled at him softly. "He told me to tell you he'd be around tomorrow to help you with the water pump."

He nodded gently and took another bite of food. "He's welcome to fruit from our trees," he offered—a weak apology.

"I think he wanted some of his own."

Well, that was nice. At least he didn't want everything that was Charlie's.

Author Note: Of all the characters in this story, I think Charlie is my favorite. Aging is such an odd and natural process. No one really knows how they might deal with aging and a serious illness until they are in the midst of it. I hope as I get older and older and older, and hopefully not sicker and sicker and sicker, that I can remember Charlie and how he—with gruff, grace, and love—dealt with what he was dealt.

Chapter 8: She Loved the Way He Loved Her

Kendal could tell from his breathing that he was now asleep. She knew it was hard for him to get comfortable enough in their bed to fall asleep. Somehow, it was easier for him to doze in his old leather recliner than anywhere else. But she insisted, each night, that she help him to their bed and not just because she wanted him there, which she did, but because she felt it couldn't be good for him to sit so much. Surely his body should shift about. He still managed, most days, to make it to the beach. He flatly refused to consider shipping in some sort of lift from the States, those slow-rising chairs for the stairs that they showed on TV. Said he'd rather leap off the veranda than sit on some goddamned chair to transport him to the sand. Why hadn't they considered his age when they built the house? Up on ten feet of piles, the house was cool and protected from storm surges but impractical for those with limited mobility. Somehow, nine years ago, he wasn't old—would never get old.

She sighed and turned to him in the dark. His face was not discernible, but she pictured it as it had been the first time she'd seen him sleep: lean and firm, slight crow's feet near his eyes, a stubble of a beard—brown mixed with gray—a cowboy sort of handsome—a sailor, a fisherman. At first, their relationship had been rather startling. She'd liked him right away, accepted his friendship. It was not just his kindness toward her that she'd appreciated. She'd appreciated the hesitant warmth of his smile, the sincerity and the infrequency of his laughter, and the way his eyes reminded her of the sea. And then, as they walked lazily along the dusty roads of Hopkins, the love he felt for the village infused her, repairing the disconnect and the months of near isolation. Her overwhelming urge to keep moving eased away as she allowed him to ease away her loneliness, as she allowed him to ease her back into society.

And if that wasn't startling enough, their friendship—which had not been just a friendship in his eyes—had twisted into something else. She'd known him only about a week. They'd been on his sailboat, skimming along between the barrier reef and the shore—the beautiful islands, called cays, to the starboard, the Maya Mountains off the port side. She'd sat near him as his hands lightly held the wheel so that the wind would not blow away their words, and she was laughing at something he'd said. Suddenly, his lips were against her open mouth, both his hands leaving the wheel as they held firmly onto her shoulders; and instead of flinching from this sudden intrusion, she'd leaned into it. As the boat listed gently leeward, she'd brought her hands to his back and kissed this man, who could have been her father. She'd kissed this man, who felt good in her arms, who'd begun to laugh at most of her jokes, whose entire face lit up at her very existence—whose entire *world* lit up at her very existence. And she'd loved the way he loved her—fell in love with the way he loved her. And then, without much ado, she'd fallen in love with him.

She was never able to picture him as a lawyer, which he claimed to be before he'd left it all behind. Not even a Matlock kind of lawyer but a corporate tax lawyer. She'd never seen him in a suit, never intended to. She would chop his body up in little pieces and feed him to the crocodiles before she'd let anyone bury him in a suit. It had been rolling around in her head a lot lately—his death. She felt it bearing down on her, and there was no way to get out of its way, and it terrified her.

She could just see them sweeping in from the States, tripping in their high heels, falling into the potholes—those bitches that hated her, bearing plastic bags of suits and ties, and she'd be powerless in her grief to stop them. She would try to talk to Charlie about it. He'd have to write it down in a lawyerly sort of way so she could just show the paper to Claire and Julie. Then she would throw one hell of a party, with music and games and punta dancing. Most of the village would come, and they would drink rum and beat drums and eat fish and cassava bread until the sun rose over the sea. And at some point in the festivities, she would burn those suits in one big bonfire on the beach.

She rolled over onto her back and then onto her other side and eased herself off the bed. A quick trip to the bathroom, and then she headed for the beach. It was just past eleven, and the early moon was a bright sliver against the dark sky. It was slightly chilly now, and her light nightshirt was not quite enough in the slight breeze that had kicked up. She headed back up the beach, toward town, but then stopped after fifty yards or so and leaned against the rough folds of her favorite palm. It was an old tree, thick and bent over from too many winds, so that it was almost hammocklike. If she were a smoker, it would be the perfect place to blow plumes of smoke into the sky and contemplate the universe.

She smelled him first—or more specifically, his cigarette. Then, quite suddenly, he was there, pressing his body against hers, and his lips were gently investigating her lips, his tongue slipping around the softness of her tongue. Gentle, however, was not what she wanted, so she pressed back hard against his kiss. As he met her pressure, his right hand moving to her breast, an uncontrollable moan escaped from her lips. His fingers left her breast and covered her mouth in a soft reminder. "Shhhh," he breathed in her ear, and she brought her teeth down on one of his fingers with a gentle growl. He laughed. His other hand shifted away from her back and down to her thigh, where it pushed its way up under the nightshirt, finding nothing but the warm expanse of her skin, and then back down to the hot wet folds of anticipation. Then it was gone—his hand—as he pulled on the string of his sweatpants, freeing himself to explore her fully. It was almost embarrassing how quickly her body responded. But then, when things had slowed, he shifted her body from the tree and into the soft sand, where he could take his time. He didn't say a word—never did—this one act he took on with the concentration of silence. And there, on the soft sand of Belize, with a crescent smile of a moon peering down on her, she celebrated his hardness, his softness, the silky pleasure of his hair, and had to bite his shoulder softly to keep from flaunting her indiscretion to all of Hopkins Bay.

Author Note: This is the part of the story where many of the members of my writers' group started to feel uncomfortable with Kendal, becoming slightly judgmental and self-righteous regarding her behavior. I remember feeling a little annoyed with them and wanting to tell them to be patient, that each chapter builds upon the next and within each chapter, the characters will grow in depth. But I realize now that I should have been thrilled—thrilled because they already cared enough about these characters to judge them and desire certain behaviors. The key to writing any character-driven story is to engage—even if that engagement leads to throwing their reading device across the room! But please don't; phones, computers, and Kindles are expensive!

Chapter 9: Looking Awesome in a Wet Suit

Charlie woke up when there was just a hint of pink on the flat end of the ocean. He sat up a bit in bed, careful not to wake Kendal, and watched through the large glass window of their bedroom as the sun sneaked into view. The rays slipped across the sea, onto the sand, and eased through the window. He glanced down toward Kendal and saw that she was watching him. His mouth softened to a smile.

"It's going to be a beauty of a day," he told her. She sat up and scooted under his arm, her head leaning against his chest, and peered, along with him, out the window. He watched, with her rough tufts of hair pressed into his skin, until the bright rays of the sun became too much to bear.

They drank coffee on the veranda and swatted absently at the mild onslaught of sand flies. "Breakfast?" she asked.

He shook his head. "Not yet."

She stood. "Then I'll be back in a little bit." And she left for her early-morning walk. He watched as she came into view from under the house and then strolled to the water. He admired her long tan legs and the sway of her light cotton shirt—one of his old shirts—as she bent down to retrieve some treasure from the sand. She turned and smiled and waved up to him before heading down the beach toward Hamanasi Dive Resort.

The air was still, with no humidity; the sea was a shimmering blue mirror. Small terns strutted ahead anxiously at her approach but never took flight, as they were not quite sure of her intentions. Kendal studied the fresh array of unmatched shoes, coconuts, plastic bottles, brown clusters of seaweed, copious amounts of green seagrass, shattered unidentifiable pieces of plastic, neatly sliced halves of oranges with their guts sucked clean, plastic spoons and forks, the severed head of a pineapple, driftwood of every shape and size—all of which had found their way to the shoreline. She looked up from the sand and shaded her eyes to the sun.

The movements on the pier of Hamanasi could only be his movements, and as she drew near, she admired the tight, ropey strength of his arms as he hoisted the scuba tanks onto the boat and into their wooden brackets. His wet suit was loose around his waist, leaving his chest bare and his legs pressed into the black silky neoprene. The flap of the top of his wet suit sadly masked his lovely derriere, but she knew it well, and her imagination was enough. She made her way onto the pier and almost to the boat before he spotted her, and she answered the broad smile that erupted on his face with one of her own.

"Morning," he said, holding the tank in midair to take her in, and then easily swung the tank into place. "I've got a pretty-full boat this morning, but there's still room for you. Want to come along? It's been awhile since you dove. Diving's gonna be awesome. It's like glass at the reef also."

"Can't." She sat on the rough deck of the pier and leaned against one of the wooden pylons. "I've got to get some work done today. I've got a lot of orders."

He nodded and reached for the next tank. "How's Charlie? Is he doing okay? I haven't forgotten about the pump. No dive this afternoon. Did you tell him I'd be by?"

"You look awesome in your wet suit. You know that, right?"

"Almost everyone looks awesome in a wet suit." He laughed.

"Are you kidding me? That is so not true!"

"Morning, Kendal." They turned to Melvin's approach. He was still on the sand and heading toward them with a large bag of gear—looking awesome in his wet suit. His cornrows were tiny, neat, straight lines against his scalp, falling into short strands of twisted dreadlocks at his neck. Even from this distance, Kendal admired the straight white flash of his teeth against his darkness—the smooth dark skin tight against the prominent bones of his face.

She smiled and waved at him before turning back toward Aaron. "Charlie's feeling well this morning. He's expecting you."

Melvin stepped onto the pier, and she turned her attention once more to him. "You look like a glistening Greek god in that wet suit!" she called out to him.

"Don't I know it!"

Aaron's laughter felt like silk to her ears. "You see," he said, pointing at Melvin as he made it to the boat, "even a big ugly mug like Melvin looks good in a wet suit."

Melvin threw the gear bag hard at Aaron, who caught it with delight. Kendal watched as the two men finished stowing the gear, placed the regulators on the first half of the tanks, and double-checked the BCDs. They were still putting the final touches on the preparations when the first of the divers from the resort started showing up.

Kendal took them in. It was a usual crew, a mixture of young adventurers and middle-aged hopefuls. She could tell, with just a quick critique, who was a seasoned diver and who was nervous as hell. Their accents gave them away as a mixture of Americans and Canadians. And she was, of course, correct—not everyone looked awesome in a wet suit. She didn't miss the looks the women—even the men—gave Aaron as they took in their head divemaster. Once he started speaking in his beautiful fast-talking accent, she could almost see the women swoon with a combination of desire and awe, sporting deep wrinkles of concentration as they tried to follow his instructions. This was the man that would lead them into the deep, their very lives his responsibility.

She saw him glance toward shore, knowing he was looking for Walter, their captain; and not seeing his approach, he started reviewing basic safety hand signals. He worked his way to his favorite fish-identification signals. When he sliced his hand against his forehead, the hand signal for shark, his eyes caught hers, and he flashed a smile just for her. Some of the women followed his gaze, and taking her in... they knew.

"Ahh, here's our captain," Aaron said as he spotted Walter strolling through the coconut palms and across the sand as if there wasn't an entire boat of divers waiting. "We'll talk more once we're at the first site."

Kendal stood up as they readied the boat for departure. She waved softly as the boat eased away from the dock. Then she brought her hand vertical against her forehead and yelled, "Tiger shark! They love Canadians!" and watched as Aaron's face, getting smaller by the moment, burst into laughter. She imagined, as soon as his laughter was spent, he'd yell over the noise of the boat to his crew of divers, "She's just kidding. We haven't lost a diver to a tiger shark in over a week now!"

Author Note: For such a tiny little country, generally compared to the size of Massachusetts, the diversity of its topography and ecology is staggering, consisting of tropical rainforests, mangrove forests, pine forests, rivers, mountains, savannas, and coast. It is also home to the second-largest coral reef in the world. The jungle and the sea are the two places I love the most. My last novel, Legend of the Lost Ass, *explored primarily the Maya culture. The modern Maya still largely inhabit the interior jungles. In* The Vast Clear Blue, *I slip more into the sea. The coastal regions of Belize are where the Garinagu (called Garifuna as individuals) eventually took up residence in 1802. Garifuna Settlement Day is celebrated on November 19. Historically, the Garinagu were fishermen, living strictly off the land and sea. As the modern world has touched Belize and the sea has been*

commercially depleted, most of the young Garifuna now work in tourism. But one thing both the old and the young Garifuna have in common is their love and respect for the sea.

Chapter 10: Feeding the Crocodiles

After breakfast, Kendal went to her studio, which was attached to the main house but perpetually separated by a closed door. The space was small. The walls were painted a soft teal; the work areas were simple wooden structures of dark-stained wood. Even the tops of the tables were made of wood. Not that it mattered, as the countertops were barely visible under the dusty cutting machines, stone polishers, piles of large and tiny colorful stone, fine slivers of silver, plastic organizers, vats of cleaning liquids, heaps of paper orders, innumerable pieces of half-finished work, stacks of design sketches, and a fine coat of white powder adorning everything. Large windows faced the water, so that if Kendal chose to look up from her work, she was confronted by an endless sea.

The room was light and airy in spite of the dust and the chaos of just too many things. Anyone else might get swallowed up, but this was Kendal's fine-tuned chaos. She could find, within moments, that special piece of blue topaz she'd ordered from Germany lying in a pile of colorless gems or that chunk of lovely green agate she'd managed to procure. There was a system to the madness, a certain protocol on which pieces received priority; and it wasn't always rated by the price she demanded, which was also rather arbitrary.

She didn't give the room a second look but went directly to her workstation.

She picked up the fine silver bracelet she was working on and studied the intricate pattern of stone inlayed in the silver. This was one she must get done. This week, if possible, so she'd have time to guarantee its arrival in the US before its recipient's wedding day. All the stones were cut; now there was the arduous but soothing task of placing each tiny sliver of stone near its perfect partner. She pushed the tiny earphones into her ears, turned on the iPod, sat down, and was lost in her world.

Charlie read on the veranda for an hour before he fell asleep, his book slipping from his fingers and dropping gently to the concrete floor. It was some time later when he woke and felt a need to see her—to watch her work. He shuffled into the house, stiffer than normal due to the hard wooden chairs on the veranda. He knocked gently on the door before he opened it. He found her across the room, sitting on a stool, hunched over the counter, her dreads falling over her face, her feet propped up on the highest rung of the stool, so that she reminded him of a crazy bird perched on a small rock. An empty chair was nearby, a tiny tray of bright-colored stones laid out before her, a neat row of metal hand tools within reach. When she glanced up from her work, he asked with a look. She smiled a welcome, so he entered her domain and sat in the empty chair—a chair meant only for him.

He watched with his usual fascination, the tip of her tongue slipping out from between her lips as she lifted the impossibly small slices of colored stone with jeweler's forceps, dipping them into the glue and gently maneuvering them into places that only she understood. The pattern of this particular piece was one of her more intricate mosaics. He remembered her earlier pieces, the ones she'd had stuffed in her backpack the day she'd first strolled into town. They came nowhere close to what she was capable of now. And with the arrival of the Internet, she had quite an international following. Very few of her things were sold here in Belize. The resorts stocked a small supply of earrings and bracelets and necklaces, but where she made her money was in places like LA, New York, and Paris. Not that it was possible to make a lot of money when it took her at least a month, from start to finish, to complete any one piece. It was not the sort of work you could do for more than a few hours at a time.

He watched her for about fifteen minutes and was about to get up and return to his book when she reached up and popped the earpieces out of her ears. They dangled like tiny white snakes from the waist of her shorts as she said, without looking up from her work, "We need to talk."

The words hit him, and he feared he might fall off his chair. His fingers, of their own accord, secured their grip on the armrests. She sent a painful glance his way and then was moved to abandon her work. She stood and paced about the room. His eyes followed the progress of her despair, his own fear mounting. He shook his head. *Don't say it!* The words boomed through his head. He did not mean it last night; he didn't want to know. They did not need to talk! He opened his mouth to say something, anything, but, oh dear God, she'd begun to clutch her chest and now was doubling over in pain. He made his way to her and clasped her balled-up body to his chest. She was gasping for breath, and he squeezed just as hard as his old arms could squeeze.

"Kendal, oh, Kendal," he soothed. "Do you need me to get you one of your pills?" He felt her shake her head, and then she found her voice.

"I can't do it!" she gasped. And she was crying now.

"It's okay. You don't have to. You don't need to. We don't need to talk." He tried to squeeze her just a little tighter.

"I can't."

"I don't need to know."

"I can't chop you up and feed you to the crocs!"

What? "What?"

"I won't see you in a suit! You have to tell them! You have to tell them!"

"I'm sorry—I don't understand."

"I can't stop it. I can't stop it. It's coming at me like a slow train, and I won't see you in a suit!"

"A suit?"

"Dead! Dead in a suit!" She almost screamed the words, but then he understood.

"No. No suit." His words were soft, and he pushed his hand through the thickness of her hair. He wished he could say no to the death part, but that was out of his control. "I'll talk to them. I'll write it down. We'll figure it all out." His knees were beginning to ache, and he had serious doubts whether he'd be able to right himself from his squatting position, but he held her while she cried until she was done and calm again.

Author Note: Crocodiles sound scarier than alligators but are in fact much more timid than gators and thus less likely to turn you into a snack. That being said, the Sittee River, which runs very close to our house, is not a place you will ever find me taking a dip!

Chapter 11: Already Packed for Somewhere Warm

Mark was becoming accustomed to waking up on the beach, but this particular morning, there was a total stillness to the air, and the sand flies were having an eating frenzy under the sheet he found wrapped around his body. Or at least that's what it felt like—that he was being eaten alive. He slapped at his skin, making his head pound, and eased his body vertical, but still, the nausea hit him hard. He made it as far as the nearest beach chair and wrapped himself up like a mummy in the sheet. His eyes burned as he peered out onto a perfect azure sea.

What the hell was he doing to himself? Well, he knew—he knew exactly what he was doing to himself. He had learned all about how the body metabolizes alcohol when he was studying pharmacy at Ohio State. In his five years at Kenny Drugs, how many Rxs for Antabuse had he filled? Not to mention all the meds he'd dispensed for diazepam or chlordiazepoxide, knowing, as he handed the bags to the shaking hands of red-eyed people, that it was more than anxiety he was treating. But damn, he sure could go for a beer about now—just to help settle his stomach.

He sat back and pushed his hand through his hair. As the fuzzy memories of last night focused in his brain, he closed his eyes with a deep sigh. What had he been thinking? Well, he hadn't thought—that was pretty obvious. Kendal was married. Not available—at least, not to him. Then there was Aaron. Was she available to Aaron? He reopened his eyes and stared miserably at his pillow, sitting abandoned on the beach.

"Did you sleep here last night?" asked a pleasant female voice. He looked up and squinted into the sun. She was close and smiling down at him, and Mark could appreciate, even in his compromised state, that she was young and beautiful.

His face broke into his most welcoming smile, and he barely noticed the shot of pain the movement caused. "Apparently so." He laughed.

She let her gaze linger just a moment on his face, and then she turned to the sea. "It's an incredible morning."

"Yes," he said, his eyes not leaving the dark flow of her hair and the way it relaxed against the swell of her breasts. "Are you staying around here?"

That smile again as she turned his way. "Yes, right up the beach at Whistling Seas, with my girlfriends." Then her face fell. "I only have two days left. Back to cold New York State. And you? Where are you from?"

"Well, you know, Ohio, I guess…"

"When do you have to go home?

Mark wasn't sure how to answer that, so he said, "I was just about to go get some coffee. Would you like some?"

"That would be great." She smiled. "My friends are still sleeping, and I haven't had a thing yet."

"Okay." Mark managed not to flinch at all as he stood up and flung his sheet onto the sand. "Have a seat," he said as he indicated the chair next to his. "I'll be right back."

He made his way quicker than he would have thought possible toward Yugadah, deciding not to take the time to make a pot in his room but to go directly to the restaurant—which didn't open until noon—and beg Cordelia for some coffee. The door was open, and he made his way into the restaurant in search of Cordelia. She looked up from her seat in the back of the kitchen, her substantial body draped over the stool, and smiled.

"Do you think…?" He glanced at the coffeepot. "Is there any way I could steal two cups of coffee from you?"

She set down the potato she was peeling and wiped her wet hands on her floral skirt. "Two?"

He grinned. "That's right."

"Praise the Lord!" Cordelia matched his grin. She poured him two steaming mugs. "You know I can't say no to you."

"Yeah. Well, hopefully she'll feel the same way."

Cordelia's warm laughter filled the place. "Good luck to you!"

He shrugged his shoulders slightly. "Hey, stranger things have happened." And pushed open the screen door with his back.

He was back at the beach in less than five minutes, before this incredible creature could slip away. "There you go." He tilted his head and smiled as he handed her a mug. "I'm Mark, by the way."

"Pattie."

"It's great to meet you," he said as he sat next to her and took the life-giving liquid into his mouth. He was trying to think of something profound to say when she spoke first.

"So, you never answered me. How long are you staying in Belize?"

He turned to her and smiled. He took another sip of coffee before he said, "Well, now, that's an interesting story." He turned back to the sea and began. "You see, I'm a pharmacist in Columbus. And there was this pharmacy conference in Orlando. Right on the Disney property. And I thought, what a great place to take my girls. I have two daughters, you see, five and six. But my—" And he paused and turned his face back to Pattie, who was smiling with interest. "Wife… Cathy, well, she won't hear of taking the girls out of school, as if missing a few days of first grade and kindergarten will keep them out of Harvard or something." He laughed, and Pattie did also. "So." He looked up to the sky and thought. "I guess a little over a week ago, I decide to go on my own.

I pack a big bag of shorts and sandals and bathing suits, a couple decent shirts in case I actually show up at a CE course or something, and head off to the airport. I make my first connection, no problem." He had her total attention, and Mark began to pick up steam. "So I'm in Pittsburgh now, just a little farther north, because God knows they can't fly you in the direction you want to go, and for some reason that only the airline god knows, I have to fly to Chicago. Even farther frigging north!" Pattie laughed, and he joined her. "Well, at first, the flight to Chicago is delayed, and this goes on for an unreasonable amount of time." He stopped and took a sip of coffee. "So I'm sitting for hours in the airport, and I'm already missing Cathy and the girls, when the flight's canceled due to weather. So... no problem, I think, surely there's a flight from Pittsburgh directly to Orlando. Well... surely there isn't, at least, not one I can get onto before I'm forty or something, so I just say fuck it! I'm going home. There's a whole other mess to get my luggage, but that's all finally sorted out. And it's late now, so I don't bother calling home, 'cause everybody's asleep by now."

He stopped, because this was the part of his story where almost everyone saw where this was going, and he wanted to stretch it out a bit. He smiled reassuringly at Pattie and kept up the tempo. "So I finally get back to Columbus, luggage remarkably in hand. It's, like, one o'clock in the morning when I pull into my garage. I'm real quiet so's not to wake anyone. First, I go to Missy's room. She's sleeping in this tight little ball, and I just have to stretch her out and hug her, you know?" Mark looked at Pattie and blinked hard a few times before rubbing his forehead and bringing a smile back to his face. "Next, I tiptoe into Tracey's room, step on some damn toy, scream out in pain, but she doesn't wake up—even when I kiss her little face...

"So anyway, a quick trip to the bathroom, and I'm back in the hall. I start taking off my clothes before I get to the bedroom—you know, trying to keep quiet and all. And I remember thinking: maybe Cathy might be up for a little welcome-home fun, so I take everything off and slip into our room. Well, it's dark as hell, but I know where everything is. I find the bed, no problem, but it's one of those massive king-sized monsters, and I can't seem to find my wife!"

Mark had to interrupt his story again because he was laughing so hard. He caught his breath and then continued. "So I'm reaching around in the dark, you know, sliding my hand across the sheets, and finally, I feel the warmth of her body, so I ease my hand up to her chest, but damn! The size of her breast is about right, but it's covered with hair!"

At this point, almost everyone he'd told the story to in Belize would be laughing like hell, but he glanced at Pattie through his own tears of laughter, and she wasn't laughing at all. Her mouth was slightly open in disbelief, and her eyes were not amused. He was way too into it to stop now, and from the look on her face, he already knew he'd blown any chance he might have had with her. There was nothing to do but go on. But he wasn't laughing anymore. "So I can't get to the light fast enough, and I scream—just like in the movies—and then they scream, and then Cathy, just as cool as hell, leans over my good friend Bob's fat fucking body and says, 'Mark, we didn't expect you home so soon.'"

He wiped again at his tears, which were perhaps not just from laughter, and looked Pattie directly in the eye as he said, "So, you see... my bags were already packed for somewhere warm."

She set her coffee down and blinked at him. "So you just left?" He nodded. "That night? Your wife? Your kids? Your job?"

"My bags were already packed," he offered weakly.

"Does she even know where you are?" she asked, shaking her head incredulously.

"I texted her and told her where I left the car at the airport," he said a bit defensively.

She narrowed her eyes, her lips pursed in an unbecoming way, and nodded ever so slightly. She opened her mouth to say something, changed her mind, and slapped at a sand fly on her leg. Mark looked away, bit his lip gently, and pushed back his anger. What right did this woman have to judge him? And so harshly. He was, after all, the victim in all of this.

Pattie stood up and smiled faintly. "Well, thanks... you know, for the coffee." She shrugged slightly. "And good luck." She was gone, back down the beach. Mark's head fell into his hands. Damn! He could really go for a beer about now.

Author Note: In this chapter, why Mark finds himself in Belize "telling everybody everything" is the scenario I came up with after we met that stranger in the sedan in search of a waterfall. While certain things are predictable and maybe even inevitable, what makes fiction so wonderful are the endless possibilities and, as a writer, when the character or the storyline surprises even me. There comes a point in character-driven fiction where the characters take over, and that is the point the writing becomes almost effortless—as long as I remain true to my characters.

Chapter 12: Star-Crossed Lovers

They ate a late lunch on the veranda. The sand flies had dispersed, despite the lack of breeze, and the day was all that Charlie had predicted. Kendal could tell that he was still feeling well. One of his good days, but the wrinkle of worry on his forehead was a concern. She knew he wanted to ask—knew that he was wrestling with the knowledge that she hated to talk about it and his desire to find out how she was doing. Kendal brought her hand down on his and smiled what she thought was a reassuring smile and said, "I'm doing okay," hoping to end it there. But she could tell she'd failed to convince him of anything, which made matters all the worse, so she stood up and cleared away the empty plates.

Kendal lingered in the kitchen. She looked down at her shaking hands and clasped them together. There would be no more inlaying of stone today, and it frustrated her. She had hours more to go on the bracelet. She never should have agreed to the deadline—she didn't mesh well with deadlines. She wrapped her arms across her chest and trapped her hands in her armpits. She bent down slightly, closed her eyes, and forced herself to breathe. The more she thought about it, the worse it became, so that it was a great relief to open her eyes at the sound of his laughter, look up, and see Aaron with her husband on the veranda. Perhaps the sight of the two of them together, laughing, would have made most people freak; but it had quite the opposite effect on her, and she immediately felt the shift, as if all the world had just tilted back into place. She made her way across the room and called out through the open glass French doors, "Would you like a sandwich, Aaron?"

"No thanks. I'm good." And his smile did not linger on hers.

"Beer?"

"Stop trying to ply me with food and alcohol," he laughed. "Your wife's trying to distract me from the work we need to do," he said to Charlie.

"Yes, she's quite a distraction." He laughed softly in return.

Kendal watched as Charlie struggled to stand, and she forced herself not to come to his aid. She noted, as the two men made their way down the veranda stairs to the utility room under the house, that Aaron did not offer Charlie a hand. But he slowed his frenetic movement as her husband stepped carefully down the steps and stayed with him. He was prepared to be needed.

Kendal cut some larger pieces of stone and checked her email for orders, sent a few replies out, and then the day was calling to her. She located her floppy bright-green hat and her large yellow sunglasses. She poured some iced tea for the men and headed for the utility room. Aaron's laughter reached her ears as she made her way down the stairs. She entered the door of the utility room to find Aaron on his knees, well surrounded by water pump guts. Charlie sat on a chair nearby, and Aaron was, of course, chattering away. He stopped when he saw her and sat down on the concrete floor, wiping the sweat from his brow with one hand and taking her offering of the icy drink with his other. Kendal handed the other to Charlie as she said, "I think I'll take the kayak out for a spin. You guys want anything else before I go?"

Charlie looked up at her from his chair. There seemed to be a question somewhere in his look, but he said, "We're good. Isn't that right, Aaron?"

"We're good," he agreed.

Kendal almost had the boat to the surf when she saw him, a long ways up the beach, but she could tell, even from this distance, that he was lost in despair. She let go of the boat and studied the slouching figure peering south. Was he looking at her? Or beyond, toward False Sittee Point? It was possible that he was peering even farther south to Placencia—remembering some moment, years ago, when his wife and he had splashed in the sea of some sort of hope. He'd shown her a photo once, from their honeymoon, Cathy tan and smiling on the white sand, the Caribbean sparkling blue behind her, the darkness of her long, straight hair a contrast against the green-blue sea. She was a beautiful woman, and her smile had the appearance of love; but it was just a snapshot out of time, and time had a way of shifting reality. And then, of course, reality had a way of not being real.

Kendal tilted her head in acceptance and began to walk. As she grew closer, his gaze altered, and there was no doubt that he was watching her approach. "I'm sorry," Mark called before she should have been able to hear him.

"Don't be stupid!" she called back.

"No. Really. I'm so sorry."

She was closer now, but she let the distance close before she responded. "Hey," she said softly, "you can't help it. You've got that whole penis thing going on that messes with your brain."

He laughed and nodded his head. "It's true."

She lifted up her sunglasses so he could see her sincerity. "I'm going out in the kayak. Come with me."

His face scrunched up in painful consideration and then settled into gratitude. "Okay."

Kendal sat in the front and let him steer. They eased out of the soft surf and into the calm. "Which way, my dear?" he asked.

"South, James, south!" She set her paddle across the boat, placed her feet on either side of the bow, and sat back.

"Hey! What are you doing?"

"I'm a princess!"

"Yeah! You're something, all right. Now I know why you wanted me to come along."

"For your big, strong muscles!" she sang out and laughed. "Faster, please." She closed her eyes to the sensation of forward motion and relished the kind rays of the sun against her legs. They progressed in silence. Turning her head to the right, she watched the shoreline float by, first Hamanasi and then the pretty little beach houses of Jaguar Reef Resort, nestled among the palms. The white sandy beach ran into the green roughness of the red mangroves, which grabbed at the shoreline with their countless grasping arms. As they closed in on False Sittee Point, the water grew shallow, and she was forced to raise herself from her throne and watch the amazing floor of the sea slip by. She picked up her paddle and eased into Mark's movement.

His light words flowed forward. "I screwed up last night and then again this morning." And he laughed at his own ineptness.

"Oh yeah?" She laughed. "Whatever did you do this morning?"

"Told this beautiful woman—that I'm pretty sure I had a chance with—my messed-up story."

Kendal giggled merrily. "It's not exactly a 'come have sex with me' kind of story."

"You think?"

She keeled over with pleasure, hugging her knees as she laughed. "We need to get you laid!" She pointed her paddle his way, tapping him gently in the chest with the blade. "That's what I'm going to do! I'm going to get you laid!"

"Good luck with that," he said dryly.

She poked the blade deeper into his chest. "It's what you need. Boost up the old confidence."

He grabbed the blade. "Cut it out! I'll toss you to the sharks!"

She withdrew her weapon. "You wait! It's gonna happen!"

Mark stopped paddling as they reached the sandy bar of False Sittee Point. "Let's look around a bit." They stepped out of the kayak and tied the bow to an arm of a mangrove. The crystal-clear water, which lapped halfway up their calves, was as warm as a perfect summer bath. They stepped gently so as not to disturb their view of the watery world. "There!" Mark pointed, and they watched as the small stingray floated away.

"What's this little guy up to?" Kendal asked as she pointed to the small hermit crab walking with definite purpose across the sandy bottom. They watched in silence as he scuttled through his own wet world. Out a little deeper, the ocean floor became covered with waving blades of grass—and there, nestled bright against the green, were two large red starfish, one bright, one dull; and they were close, their thick arms entwined. "Star-crossed lovers," Kendal whispered.

Mark's laughter rolled across the water. "You don't know that. Maybe they're meant to be together."

"No way. It's doomed."

They returned to the boat and made their way farther south along the much-smaller bay located between False Sittee Point and Sittee Point. The entire bay had been purchased, years ago, by a US developer, and now the pretty, white shoreline was dotted with the construction of single homes and a few small resorts. It saddened Kendal to see the building—the destruction of the tall, stately black mangroves, which were protected yet not protected by the Belizean government. And now there was the new, even-larger development north of Hopkins, bracketing this tiny village with foreign investment. Would the heart, the tradition, the Garifuna culture of Hopkins ultimately survive? Or would the village be slowly squeezed away by the progression of greed? But how could she dare to entertain such thoughts? Hadn't she and Charlie claimed their own little piece of paradise? Weren't they a part of the intrusion? So how could she deny these people's right to the gift of Belize? But some of these homes were unnecessarily massive concrete structures, built on clear-cut lots, with no preservation of the natural foliage—a reproduction of Florida. If they wanted Florida, why not take Florida?

"Look at some of these places," she told Mark.

"Yeah, they're nice."

"Nice? It looks like Florida!"

"Florida's nice."

"You're a stupid jerk!" she laughed.

"Yes. And your point?"

She laughed again. "My point is, look at some of these places. Could they not save a single tree? And what's up with that place?" She pointed to the large pink concrete structure, with a massive white staircase in the center of the house, opening up to the ocean.

Mark looked at the home. "Yeah, what's wrong with it?"

"What's wrong with it? Look at those stairs. All that pink. It's a big, giant vagina!" She collapsed into laughter, and Mark joined her. "The way those stairs are made. Wide at the beginning and tighter—you can only hope—the further you go."

"Oh my God." Mark howled with laughter. "You're a freak. Who thinks like that?"

Kendal continued to laugh. "Really! Look at it. You can't tell me it doesn't look like a vagina."

She watched Mark study the inviting pink structure. "Okay. Okay. I'll give you that," he admitted through his laughter. "But do you have to say that sort of stuff out loud?"

Kendal was taken over by joy—the joy of laughing on a blue, blue sea. She had to lean against her paddle as she laughed. She imagined the notes of their abandonment to laughter winging across the sea, bouncing off the dark expanse of the wings of the magnificent frigate birds sailing over their heads, and reaching the ears of Charlie and Aaron as they worked. When they looked up at the resonance of joy, what would they think? And what would they believe?

Author Note: The Belizean coast near Hopkins is made up of several small bays punctuated by peninsulas. The undeveloped sandy knolls are where the red mangroves thrive, creating beautiful, strange forests. The long prop and drop roots extending from these trees have given them the name "walking tree" and provide sanctuary for both marine and land-loving wildlife. The waters surrounding the peninsulas are just inches deep and are teeming with creatures such as starfish, hermit crabs, rays, small fish, snails, worms, seagrass, and tiny conches!

Chapter 13: Avoiding the Shark

Charlie sighed as he listened to Aaron's endless talk and watched with frustration as the young man tried to fit the pieces of the pump back together. How many times had he, over the years, dismantled and repaired this pump in half this time? He itched to get his hands in there, to shove Aaron aside and put it all back the way it was, only fixed and no longer leaking. But he knew, if he made it to the floor, that he would not be able to rise without Aaron's aid, and he'd be damned if he was going there.

"This stupid fat American..." Aaron was smiling as he talked. "No matter how many times I go fetch him and signal to him to stay with the group—preferably behind me!—this fucking guy keeps taking off. So we're about halfway through the dive when I look around, and I can't find him! The fucker has disappeared again!" Aaron laughed as he stopped talking for a moment and shifted the bladder of the pump into place. "I look back at Melvin and give our sign for 'Have you seen the shithead?'—you see, there's almost always one in every dive—and he tells me no. Now I'm really getting annoyed and maybe a little worried, 'cause even though this guy deserves to get himself tangled up on a piece of coral or something, I don't need the grief, and he's disrupting the dive. Pissing the others off too—"

"Be careful how tight you screw that in," warned Charlie.

Aaron smiled at Charlie. "Yeah, I know. So, finally, I spot him, thirty yards ahead and a good twenty feet above the group. The motherfucker is just floating up there, all alone like the Goodyear Blimp. I try banging on my tank to get his attention, but he's in his own little world, and before I get the chance to go get him, out of nowhere comes this sweet little lemon shark, making a beeline right for this fat fucking fool!"

Charlie couldn't help himself; he began to laugh along with Aaron.

"Now, I'm not worried, but I see this guy take in this shark coming right at him, and even from that distance, I could tell he was shitting his wet suit! It was all I could do not to laugh my regulator right out of my mouth. Of course, the shark, hardly more than three foot long, veered off to the left and disappeared. But I'll tell you what! Fatso was right there with me, holding on to my flipper the rest of the dive!"

Charlie laughed. And even though laughter should have relieved the feeling that had been scratching on him for the last twenty-four hours, the irony of the laughter intensified the feeling. He just couldn't brush it away.

"There always seems to be just one in every dive that makes you want to scream," Aaron continued. "Every once in a—"

"How long have we known each other, Aaron?"

Aaron looked up from his work and smiled at him. "I don't know... a year and a half? Pushing two..."

Charlie narrowed his eyes in thought. "You know, I met your dad first. Down by the dock, and we started to talk. I liked him immediately. I was the one that told him about the job... at Hopkins Bay Resort. You knew that, right?"

Aaron had set down the part he had been holding and was looking at him kindly, but there was an uncharacteristic stillness to him—a waiting. "Yes, I know that."

"I miss your dad and your mom. I was sorry to see them leave."

"I miss them too."

"And you... well... you've been a godsend to me. Especially since I've been sick. Like the son I never had." Aaron's face had turned a shade toward pain, and Charlie was moved to continue. "I would do anything for you. You know that... but there's that proverbial line... in the sand, if you want... that a man—a good man—does not cross..."

"Oh, fuck." Aaron's head went down in his hands.

Now that scratch became a full-blown attack, and Charlie needed to get up and leave.

"I'm so sorry. It just sort of happened. Fuck. I don't even know what to say. I never meant to. Never again. I swear."

Charlie was up now and on his feet. "How long?" His words came out in an unbecoming croak.

Aaron glanced up at him, then his head was back in his hands. "Not long. A month? Two?" He shook his head. "Jesus, fuck, I'm sorry."

Charlie was out the door of the utility room and into the fresh air of the Caribbean. The distance to the stairs along the side of the house that led him to the safety of his home was nearly insurmountable, and he was halfway to the first step when he heard the unmistakable sound of happiness. He turned to the sea and could just see them making their way toward shore, and she was laughing with the kind of laughter that pushed all worry aside. Her head, adorned with that crazy green hat, was tilted back, her face bejeweled with the yellow of her sunglasses, and his heart surged with love and the joy of her pleasure. And then he was nearly knocked down with grief. *Oh, dear God! What had he done?*

Charlie reentered the utility room to find Aaron unmoved—his head still down in his hands as he sat on the floor. "You can't tell her I know," he said urgently.

Aaron looked up tragically. "I won't. I'll just end it. I swear."

"No! You can't. You can't change a thing." Charlie had to grasp his chest at the urgency of his words.

Aaron stood up with concern. "She won't know. It will be okay," Aaron was saying as he came closer.

Charlie grabbed the back of the chair for support. "Listen, you stupid goddamn fool! You can't change a thing. You can't end it or tell her. She won't be able to handle it. Don't you see?" Charlie could feel the sweat trickling down around his eyes, seeping onto his cheeks. "My death is like a big buzzard waiting to pick her apart." Aaron was there now, holding his arm and keeping him from falling. "If she even thought, even suspected, and…" He closed his eyes. "Goddamn it. She needs you. Don't you see? It's just waiting to pick her apart." He was leaning on Aaron now, and what he really wanted to do was to reach up to this stupid kid's neck and squeeze it till his eyes popped out.

"Okay. Okay! I get it. Jesus, Charlie, let me help you upstairs. Should I get Nurse Ruth?" They were moving slowly now, out the door and into the light.

"You understand? You see how things are?" Charlie hissed as he saw the kayak was now on shore.

"Yeah. I get it."

"Nothing can change," he insisted as he saw Kendal look up from the boat and see them. He watched as her face turned to panic, watched her drop the paddle and start to run his way, with Mark close behind.

"Charlie, I'm so sorry," he heard Aaron whisper, and suddenly, they were all there, helping him up the stairs, getting him into his chair, and fussing over him until he practically had to scream for them to leave him alone. Just leave him alone!

Author Note: I'm not sure if you've noticed this yet, but Aaron is the only one of the four major characters in this story without a direct voice; we never get in his head. I enjoy writing from multiple points of view and have done so in all my novels. I believe it's a wonderful way to add complexity and dimension to a story. But I also enjoy the challenge of making a character come alive only through his dialogue, his actions, and what others think about him. I wouldn't mind getting to know Aaron a little better! Does he miss his family in South Africa? What motivates him besides growing fruit? What got him into diving? Does he truly love Kendal? Per-

haps, by the final chapter of The Vast Clear Blue, you'll be able to come up with some ideas and questions of your own!

Chapter 14: In Search of the Jaguar

Kendal claimed that this was her favorite hike in all of Belize, and Mark was anticipating the morning hike with as much enthusiasm as he could muster. He'd tried—really, he had—to limit his alcohol intake the previous night, as it only took a few beers to ease away Ohio. But there was something about the night air of Belize and the camaraderie of the village that just plain made him thirsty. There'd been the possibility, depending on how Charlie was feeling, that the whole excursion would be scrapped, and it would've been a shame to give up a night of drinking for nothing.

It had started innocently enough. He'd gone to the Indian restaurant with Aaron, where he'd ordered a wonderful curry, so hot and spicy that his eyes and nose had run with pleasure, making the long, soothing gulps of beer a necessary addition. They'd started talking to a couple guys from Canada, the only other people in the covered outdoor eating area, which was a few steps from the sea and surrounded by palms. It seemed a bit odd—the combination of sand, palms, and curry. The restaurant itself was nothing more than a dilapidated shack, which the American health department officials and fire marshals would've had a field day with. Mark made the mistake of using the bathroom and used the beach for the rest of the evening. But the food this man made in the tiny kitchen was incredible. Everything was fresh and made-to-order; none of the vegetables or meats had ever seen the inside of a cellophane wrapping. He'd asked for hot, and boy, had the owner delivered.

The Canadians were young, college-aged men who were backpacking through Central America. They had quick smiles and a wonderful way of throwing *ehs* at the end of their sentences—just like on *Saturday Night Live*—and the four of them had sat over their beers and talked for hours about everything from snakes to tortillas. Then, late into the evening, the owner, Ravi, and the waiter, Anish, who turned out to be Ravi's brother, had joined them. Ravi had brought with him a bottle of fine, velvety whiskey and six small glasses. Ravi smelled of turmeric and cumin and sweet onions and all the incredible things he'd spent the night cooking, and the six of them had made a night of it. Mark had waited for just the right moment, when the bottle of whiskey was all but gone, to tell these fresh new sets of ears his sad and funny tale of betrayal and woe. His delivery was as fine-tuned as any seasoned stand-up comic's—he had them almost rolling off their chairs and into the sand with laughter. Even Aaron, who'd seemed edgy all evening, was laughing as if it were all brand new. And when he said the line about fat fucking Bob's hairy boobs, Ravi had laughed so hard that Mark had worried for the man.

Then the talk and the laughter had turned to all that was wrong, and all that was right, with women. Aaron, who normally didn't join Mark late into the night, began to mellow into his chair and didn't break away when it got late—had stayed right there with them until well into the second bottle of whiskey and well into the morning. So that now, only a few short hours of sleep later, it was Kendal, and only Kendal, who bounced out of the car with unabated eagerness.

"You know, we could've waited another hour or two." Mark just had to say it one more time as he eased his body out of the Tracker.

"How many times do I have to tell your lazy butt that we'll never see that jaguar that's waiting right up the trail if we don't get an early start?" chided Kendal. She studied the overhead canopy as if she expected to see a big cat staring down at her.

Aaron leaned sluggishly against the hood of the car and lit a cigarette. He blew a gentle cloud into the morning air before he said, "You know, Mark, she's never seen a jaguar. Most likely never will."

"And you're right. I never will if you don't put out that stupid cigarette and get a move on. Unbelievable. What's wrong with the two of you?" Then she was gone, walking quickly down the road to the trailhead.

Mark and Aaron watched her depart in silence. Aaron took another long drag off his cigarette then put it out on the bottom of his boot. He stuck the butt in his shirt pocket and shrugged at Mark.

"Is she really mad?" Mark asked.

Aaron laughed gently. "Nah. She never gets mad." Then he began to walk.

Mark took in the canopy bending over the narrow dirt road as he joined Aaron. This jungle, Cockscomb Basin, leaning in around him, was only a few long, bumpy miles from Hopkins, and it was a whole other world of greens and dark-brown trunks and flashes of butterflies and tiny bright flowers bursting with fragrance. As he walked, the heavy fog of alcohol and brain atrophy began to clear, and his mood lifted. It was hard to believe that he was here, surrounded by lushness, walking in the one-hundred-fifty-square-mile jaguar preserve in the middle of Belize, when there were other people shoveling snow in Ohio right now so that they could get to work. Hopefully, fat fucking Bob was up to his man-breasts in snow. And he was here, surrounded by beauty and trying to catch up to a beauty of a woman; and even if that woman could never be his, it was a hell of a thing to catch up to. Why, exactly, would he ever go back to Ohio?

He hummed the tune of "My City Was Gone" by The Pretenders, mostly in his head, as they walked, enjoying Aaron's uncustomary silence. Kendal had turned in to the jungle, and Mark stopped to read the sign at the trailhead. "Tiger Fern Trail, 2 km," it read. He was glad to see that it was only a two-kilometer hike. He could do that drunk in his sleep. Aaron caught up to Kendal and whispered something into her ear, made her laugh, and Mark fell in behind.

No one spoke, except in whispers, as the jungle took them in. Shrouded in the mist of the early-morning coolness, giant tree ferns fanned overhead. The massive cohune palms, sporting long hanging stalks of huge clusters of cohune nuts, caused Mark to pause with wonder as Aaron told him what he knew about the plant. Birds sang as they flitted among the greenery. Small lizards, flashing stripes of color, scurried through the underbrush. Mark came close but managed not to trample on the bustling highway of leafcutter ants up early and already marching along with their heavy green burdens, held high like little protest signs. He squatted on the ground and studied the miniature excavated trail all the tiny ant feet had made over time. It followed their hiking trail along for a while and then just disappeared into the forest. "That is so cool," he said, almost to himself. He looked up to see Kendal pursing her lips at him—a bright-red flower next to her face—which looked a lot like those wax lips he'd worn as a kid.

"Hot lips," Aaron told him with a soft laugh. "*Psychotria*. It's in the coffee family."

"Beautiful," he whispered.

Kendal suddenly looked up and to her right. "There!" she whispered urgently as she pointed upward. "Do you see him?" They followed her gaze. "Up high. On that branch."

Mark scanned the trees. What was he looking for?

"Oh, nice," agreed Aaron. "There's another one, up a little higher."

"Oh, yeah!" exclaimed Kendal.

"What are we looking at? Is it something that's going to eat me?" whispered Mark.

"Toucans," answered Aaron.

"Keel-billed," Kendal added. "It will only eat you if you're a fruit."

"Well, then, he'll certainly have no interest in the manly likes of me," Mark said dryly, scanning the canopy and still not finding the birds.

Kendal laughed, placed her hand on his shoulder, leaned into him slightly, and pointed with her other arm. "Over there," she said.

Mark redirected his gaze, sighting along her arm. Then suddenly, he found the first bird, rubbing its massive green-and-blue beak against the branch it perched on. He quickly located the other. "Very cool," he whispered.

They watched the birds in silence for a few minutes before continuing up the trail. They progressed slowly and silently as if each bend of the trail might reveal some wild treasure of Belize, and Kendal held on to the hope of catching a glimpse of her elusive jaguar. "It's watching us," she breathed into Mark's ear, pressing her hand against his shoulder. "Can't you feel its yellow feline eyes sizing up your back? Hear its rough panting? Its pink tongue dripping with anticipation?"

Mark felt the shiver of her words sneak up his neck. "Stop it." He really was a bit creeped out, because he *could* feel it—he could feel the entire jungle watching the approach of their intrusion. As they progressed deeper under the canopy, the trees grew taller, and they were forced to step over the buttress of broad roots snaking across the ground, being careful not to tromp on the never-ending trails of leaf-cutters.

The incline was gradual, but it wasn't all that long before Mark felt the force of gravity and the exertion of his breath. Maybe this wasn't going to be such an easy two kilometers. He reached into his small pack to remove the water bottle he'd brought and felt the subtle thud in his chest as his heart pushed around a little extra oxygen. Damn, he was out of shape. He slowed down to let his heart, which was now pounding in his ears, ease off a bit, and he watched Kendal and Aaron disappear around a bend in the trail. Then he was alone. He stopped completely and felt the eyes and the mystery and the breadth of the place—the silence and the noise—the musical sweep of the canopy, the fleeting interruption from a harsh animal call, and the crash of some forest fruit falling toward the earth. This was the moment it should appear: silently padding along on its powerful paws, stopping and watching him as his breath stayed in his throat, then disappearing into the undergrowth without a sound. And his imagination was almost enough as he turned his attention back to his task and pushed his body to catch up to his companions.

Author Note: The jungles of Central and South America were not exactly as I imagined they would be. I guess I was expecting the sort of jungle that was depicted in those old Tarzan movies, with overgrown monstrous vegetation crawling with creatures trying to maim, suck, strangle, or poison anyone foolish enough to enter. What I've learned from the countries I've visited is that the jungle is a sacred, enigmatic place. If you're incredibly patient or extremely lucky, it will share with you its secrets.

Chapter 15: Breaching Boundaries

The trail grew steeper yet, and even Kendal and Aaron were forced to slow down. "Watch where you put your hands. Make sure you're not grabbing on to a snake or a spiny bark," warned Aaron as it became necessary to pull their bodies upward.

Finally, the forest fell away as they reached the summit of this little mountain, and they took the trail to the left to show Mark the view. There was a small open structure with a picnic table overlooking Cockscomb Basin. Mark stood awed by the view.

"That's Victoria Peak," said Aaron as he pointed east. "Second-highest point in Belize. It's an awesome hike, a good three days. I did it the first year I was here. You have to go with a guide. Sleeping out in the jungle. Trekking around in the dark. Even then, I never saw a jaguar. They're nocturnal, you know," he told Mark. He smiled gently at Kendal. "Maybe... someday."

Kendal flopped down on the bench with a sigh. "If only we'd gotten here just a little earlier. Before he went off to sleep." She sighed. "They're out there. Somewhere." Kendal looked out over the top of the surrounding jungle canopy.

Mark followed her gaze. He'd read somewhere that Cockscomb Basin supported the highest concentration of jaguars in the world—around two hundred of the cats roamed the park. There were monkeys and birds, other types of cats, these strange rodents that looked like huge guinea pigs, snakes of all kinds, tapirs and funny-looking raccoon-like things, and so many other creatures he'd read about.

But as he studied the distant canopy, all he saw was a vast expanse of green.

They ate some of the peanut butter sandwiches Kendal had brought and rested in the cool of the shelter for a few minutes before Kendal stood up and announced, "Onward, men! To the falls!"

They rose obediently and followed the slight ravine down to the left and into the jungle. The trail leading to the falls was narrow and steep, with multiple switchbacks, which became tighter and tighter as they worked their way down. "I hate switchbacks," Kendal complained as she contemplated forging her own path straight down.

"Don't do it," warned Aaron. Kendal flashed him a look of disobedience. "You'll break your leg, and we'll leave you here to rot," he added, as if it would make a difference.

Mark watched as Kendal left the trail, scaling down the steep, lush decline. "Three hours," Aaron called. "That's all we have to get you to Dangriga. Once he bites you—three short hours." He turned to Mark with a smile. "Fer-de-lance, the most aggressive and poisonous snake in Central America. They have antivenom in Dangriga." And then he shrugged and continued down the trail.

Mark heard the falls well before he could make it out from the dense foliage. The last few yards were the hardest, and he was forced to grab the ropes that were tied along the trail. Then he could see the waterfall cascading into a jungle pool. It was right-out-of-a-magazine perfect, surrounded by jungle and twinkling in the morning sun. "Wow!"

Kendal was already near the pool and flashed him a smile as she pulled her shirt over her head. "Isn't it amazing?" she called, her face lost in her shirt, the smooth, sleek wonder of her stomach, her ribcage, the slightness of her bikini top. Mark almost fell on his ass in amazement. He redirected his attention to the last few feet of tricky footing, and by the time he'd reached the little pebbled shore, Kendal had disappeared into the depth of the pool. She came up with a scream, her hands reaching for the sky. "Oh my God! It's cold!" But then she was gone again, under the water and making for the falls.

Aaron and Mark watched her silently for a minute before Aaron told him, "The upper pool is better. Warmer." He stripped off his shirt and began to remove his boots and socks. Mark was moved to do likewise. But before he was done, Kendal was out of the pool and gingerly making her way across the creek and up a small path to the right of the pool that Mark would have never found on his own. He peered at the top of the falls. There was no indication that another waterfall existed. He followed Aaron up the steep path, and within minutes, they were looking at an even larger cascade and a second deep-blue jungle pool already inhabited by Kendal.

"Come on!" she called.

Mark tested the water with a toe. "It's freezing."

"You just got to go for it," said Aaron as he made his way onto the slippery rock and slid into the water with a gasp. "Fuck!" he yelled, and Kendal laughed with glee.

Mark stood on the edge with uncertainty. He really wasn't all that hot. The sun was on them, but it was still weak with morning.

"Come on," called Kendal. "It's warmer over here." She swam to the far left shore of the pool, where a soft flow of water cascaded down a red-stained slip of stone. "It's a hot spring. Well, warm, anyways." Still, Mark did not join them. "What? Are you afraid your balls are gonna drop off?" she sang.

"Well, maybe not fall off, but suck up there so far they might never come back out." And then he was jumping and hitting the icy cold, and his balls did indeed contract with shock. He burst to the surface with a primal scream that must have sent unseen monkeys plummeting from the canopy. It was unbelievable, as he floated back—with Kendal's laughter ringing through the air, with his eyes resting on the overhanging vines, with the cool sensation of the water settling around him—that he was here, in the middle of nowhere, surrounded by life in its most overpowering form and, at least for this moment, a part of it.

Kendal stayed at the upper falls while Mark and Aaron made their way back to the lower pool. Mark was cold now and wanted to retrieve his shirt, and he suspected Aaron was after a little nicotine. Aaron remained strangely silent as they made their way back, and Mark began to wonder if it was more than just the hangover that kept him from his usual prattle. They sat on the rocky edge of the pool and could just see Kendal as she sat among the falling water at the top of the falls. "She likes her water, doesn't she?"

Aaron looked up at Kendal and nodded. "She's a Pisces. You know, the fish—if you believe that shit."

Mark put on his shirt and settled onto the rocks. He pulled out the remainder of his peanut butter sandwich and longed for a beer. Aaron sat nearby and dug through his pile of clothing until he located his cigarette butt and lighter. He lit the smashed end and sucked until it was burning gently then sat back a bit and studied Kendal as she lounged upon her rock. It was peaceful and calm, with the jungle all around them, the music of the falling water. But Aaron's brooding silence was not a quiet thing, and it disrupted any peace that Mark might have savored. If Aaron had been an old friend or a brother or his wife, he might have asked what the screaming silence was all about, but instead, he said, "This place is amazing."

Aaron nodded without taking his eyes off of Kendal. Then his head came down near his knees, and his hands pulled through his wet hair. "Charlie knows," he stated. "About Kendal and me. I thought we were being so cool." His eyes flicked to Mark and then back up to Kendal. "I guess you know too."

Mark's eyes went from Aaron and then to Kendal. "Yes. It's what I assumed." He'd never seen them so much as touch; in fact, it was he that Kendal touched and flirted with. But it was he who'd been shot down flatly on the beach. And he'd known, even as he'd tried to take her for his own, that she was more than just married but already taken.

Aaron sighed unhappily and tucked a strand of his hair behind an ear.

"What's she gonna do?" Mark asked. "What's going to happen now?" *What happens once the husband knows?*

"Kendal doesn't know that Charlie knows." Aaron turned to him and added quickly, "You can't tell her."

Mark threw up his hands. "Hell. I'm not getting involved."

Aaron turned back to Kendal. "It's complicated."

"Well, it always is in these sorts of things." And suddenly, Mark was angry. How could Aaron just sleep with someone else's wife? They were friends, Aaron and Charlie, and Charlie was ill. What sort of man does that? And he pushed his drunken kiss on the beach with Kendal out of his mind as he said, "Is it just about the sex? Is that why men sleep with other men's wives?" He could see fat fucking Bob laughing and drinking beer with him while they'd watched the last Ohio State–Michigan game together. Had he been sleeping with Cathy then? Sleeping with his wife and giving him high-fives each time Ohio State scored? How, exactly, did one do that sort of thing? Mark stared at Aaron, waiting for him to say something—anything—to help him understand.

Aaron crushed his cigarette roughly against a rock until the tobacco smeared an ugly stain.

Aaron's silence was maddening. "Is it out of your control?" Mark demanded. "*Do you at least love her?*"

Aaron stood up, and with a look, he told Mark not only to fuck off but that their friendship had absolute boundaries, and those boundaries had just been breached. Mark watched as Aaron stepped neatly over the creek and disappeared up the trail leading to the upper falls.

Mark's gaze turned up to Kendal. Her eyes were closed to the sun, her head tilted back toward the sky, her dreads falling like ropes from the back of her head. He sighed, and he waited. It wasn't terribly long before her head came down and her face turned to the left. He could see the welcoming smile. She stood, her hand coming out as if reaching for a dream. Then she disappeared from view into what Mark could only assume was Aaron's arms.

Author Note: Probably one of my most memorable moments in Belize was the first time I ever set my eyes on the falls and pools of Tiger Fern Trail. I was not as strong of a hiker as I am today and remember being sweaty and exhausted as we struggled down the narrow, slippery trail. Like Kendal, it only took me moments to shed my clothes and drop into the first pool. Ah! Heaven! Years later, we met this young man at a bar. I asked him what he'd done that day. When he told me he'd done the Tiger Fern Trail, I mentioned how amazing the second falls was. When he looked at me blankly, I realized he hadn't known there was another, higher, right-out-of-Outdoor-Magazine waterfall. An opportunity lost. I'm pretty sure I wrecked his evening.

Chapter 16: Tongue Against Cheek

His chest felt warm against her wet, cold skin, and she moved with him away from the pool and into the surrounding foliage. He cupped her breast and freed it from its bondage. "Mark?" she asked as his warm mouth pressed against the coolness of her nipple.

He took his time to answer. He made his way back to her mouth and said, "That motherfucker will stay right where he is."

"Are you angry with him?" She gasped as his hand moved between her thighs.

"He's just a fucking judgmental hypocrite. That's all." Aaron's hand tightened around her leg, and he pulled her hips into his. "He wants you almost as much as I do, and yet he judges me."

She pulled away from him and gave him a wicked smile. "Hey! A threesome! What do you say?" Kendal enjoyed the look of mild reproach on Aaron's face and then had to close her eyes, air slipping through her teeth with a small hiss as his hand slid forward.

"No more talking." He pressed harder against her. "That's what I say."

Kendal's love for him was something that had never brought on insecurity. It was a comfortable thing, something he just knew—like the way his tongue fit into his mouth—not something you really ever thought about unless there was a canker sore or a piece of food between your teeth. And Aaron, well, he was more a canker sore than a flake of fish between Charlie's molars. These were the thoughts that were going through his head as he studied the card Noel had just put down. Charlie had made his way out of the house an hour or so ago, and then Noel had strolled down the beach with a deck of cards and challenged him to a game of rummy.

"Do you want the card or not, man?"

Charlie looked up from his musings to the dark, round face of his friend and shook his head. "You give me crap. You've always given me crap." He pulled a card from the deck, which was also crap, and threw away an insignificant ten of clubs. They were sitting in the shade of the house. There was just a baby's breath of breeze coming off the sea, and it was hot. Noel looked at the ten and rubbed the tight, round bulge of his stomach, something he did when he was thinking or unsure.

Charlie had met Noel years ago, when he'd had a little trouble with theft. Although Noel made his living as a fisherman, he also drew a small salary from the local police station. He was one of the few Garifuna men that Charlie could call a friend—one of the few Garifuna men that offered more than just a friendly smile and a few warm words. Noel looked at Charlie as more than just a white man with money but as someone to go fishing with, as someone, on a hot, still day, to play cards with.

"I guess I'll take your crap for now," Noel said. He was reaching for the ten when they heard the unmistakable sound of Aaron's beat-up car coming down the road. The look that flashed across Noel's face as he glanced up from the cards was not a thing that Charlie missed.

So it was with pain and a touch of embarrassment, mixed with pride and the anticipation of pleasure—his tongue slipping around in his mouth—that Charlie looked up from his own cards at the sound of Aaron slowing down and then stopping in front of the house.

Kendal stepped out of the passenger seat and shut the door of the car without a second look at its occupants. Her face bloomed into a smile when she saw them, and she moved toward them with effortless beauty. "I'm so glad to see you outside," she called before she drew near.

"Good day, Noel." And then she was there, hugging him, her wet hair pressing into the side of his face; and Charlie could smell the jungle, the animal wildness on her body—and it was with some sort of warped satisfaction that he looked up from her embrace at Aaron watching from his car and then with even greater satisfaction as the car popped into gear and disappeared in a cloud of dust.

Author Note: There are so many ways to define love, and marriage, for that matter. Is marriage about possession? Marriage certainly isn't only about love. Perhaps the strongest marriages are those in which both participants are fully formed, confident human beings where possession is minimal, and what makes the union strong is the joy of shared lives and the satisfaction of helping the other navigate their shortcomings and needs. Which brings us right to Chapter 17!

Chapter 17: Seas Shifting to Unease

The morning was cloudy and cool. The night rains had settled the dust and filled in the potholes so that there was a freshness to the air and the sound of flying mud each time a car drove by the house. Kendal sat near the surf, which was not its normal blue but a choppy gray with tiny whitecaps emphasizing the turbulence. She could see the dive boat bouncing out to the reef. It would not be a fun ride, yet once you leaned back and let your body drop into the calmness and the silence of the undersea, all unease would disappear from your stomach and your mind.

It had been late last night before she was finally able to sleep. She'd stayed up to lay the final stones of the bracelet and then wasn't able to bring her body to slumber, so that today she felt the unease as if she were bobbing on the surface, gasping for air. She wished that she could join them and sink under the disquiet, but she had to finish and send the bracelet off by the afternoon. The trip to Dangriga to FedEx the package was not something she was looking forward to, and she watched the boat's departure with a mild, achy yearning until it had disappeared into the feeble sunrise. Kendal stood up and brushed the sand from the backs of her thighs. She turned from the sea, her eyes resting on her home for a moment. She sighed and headed inside.

Kendal found Charlie already asleep again in his chair. It was not quite eight thirty—he'd been up for all of two hours. To be fair, she knew he'd also slept poorly, but still, she felt the irritation. She would like to join him in his little nap if it were not an impossibility. Sleeping had always been a chore for her. First, there was the actual falling asleep, and then there was the staying asleep. Then, on top of that, were the dreams that haunted her if the first two chores managed to be completed. So at least some of her irritation was just good old-fashioned jealousy, and the rest was her feeling of isolation—of loneliness in her own house and the tiptoeing around that loneliness.

She went quietly to her studio and spent the next hour putting the final touches on the bracelet and packaging it for mailing. She checked the time. If she left soon, she'd have no trouble making it to Tropic Air and getting it on the one p.m. flight. And if she was making the trip, there was the banking that should be done. Then it became necessary to go shopping, as there were so many more options in Dangriga than in Hopkins. One of a handful of the major towns in Belize, Dangriga was the fifth largest, with about eleven thousand people—a far cry from the thousand residents of Hopkins. Even though Dangriga was barely a blip on the radar by US city standards, it never failed to cause her stress.

Kendal breathed deeply and tried to squelch the anxiety that threatened to overtake her. But the thought of all that a trip to Dangriga entailed—her hatred of driving, the bumpy, muddy roads, the traffic and chaos of the town, the narrow, confusing streets, the armed guards and the lines at the bank, the crowded fresh-meat-and-vegetable market—was overwhelming. The whiteness of her skin attracted the needy—people wanting something from her—clustering like flies, taking everything if they had the chance. And she would be overcome by their need, wanting to give it all if she could. Saved only by innate self-preservation, she would shake her head gently and smile at the little man who tried to latch himself onto her as soon as she parked the car. "No, thank you. I'm good. I don't need any help."

And then there was the farmers' market. Which stall to buy the pineapple from? Which farmer looked more destitute, more desperate—and who was she to make that choice? She'd buy a melon from one and a bag of tomatoes from another. She'd buy the beans from the sad Maya man with no teeth, the papaya from the pregnant girl with no shoes, and fresh snapper from the fisherman with the missing fingers. And in the end, she'd be carrying so many tiny bags of hope and so unsure that she'd made even a little bit of difference that it would be impossible for her to progress from her own desperation.

Kendal clutched the FedEx package to her chest and breathed in deep gulps of dusty air from her studio and forced herself to be reasonable. It was a thing that must be done.

"Come with me to Dangriga," she said as she roused him from his sleep.

"Huh? What?"

"I have to get this bracelet off. Come with me." It was something they'd almost always done together, the shopping, the banking... and now, more and more, she was alone.

He groaned.

"Is that an 'I've been rudely awakened' groan or a 'No. Not Dangriga' groan?" she asked, tempering her anxiety and forcing a smile onto her face. She watched him blink and then study her in his half-asleep stupor.

He rubbed away the sleep from his face and smiled. "Sure. Of course."

Then her smile grew into the real thing.

Author Note: Farmers' markets in Belize, while not as elaborate or massive as in other Central and South American countries, are hubs of activity and places for vast cultural experiences. My favorite farmers' market is the one in Belmopan, the capital of Belize. You can grab anything from a pineapple to a cheap plastic toy windmill. The best meal served in all of Belize is to be had here at the open wooden structure next to the parking lot. Maya and wonderful, the stewed chicken with rice and beans is to die for. Their salbutes are fresh, crunchy, and amazing. If you go, watch out for

the veggie condiment in big glass jars on the tables; it's delicious but spicy-hot with habaneros!

Chapter 18: Navigating Potholes

She drove, as the clutch was hard for him, and she took her time through the maze of potholes. "So, you're going fishing with Mark and Aaron tomorrow," she reminded him as they turned away from the village and along the long, straight stretch of road toward the highway.

"Is that tomorrow?" He made a face. "They can take the boat and go without me."

She flashed him a look. "Why? I thought you were looking forward to it. When's the last time you've been to the cays? Don't you want to go fishing?" He shook his head. "You keep saying you want to get back out there. Catch that big old grouper with your name on it."

She tried to check her impatience. It was so tiring—him acting like he was already dead. She hit a large pothole and cussed under her breath. When he didn't readily answer, she added quietly, "You love the cays."

There was another deep sigh. "True. But I don't love the idea of spending the day with the two of them," he finally said.

She brought the truck to a near stop and turned to him. "Is there a problem I don't know about?"

He turned his head away from her, peering out at the large marsh of seagrass, and said, "No, not really. But, you have to agree that Mark's a pain in the ass."

"He's hurting. He's really looking forward to fishing with the two of you. You could help him. Male bonding and all that stuff."

Charlie sighed lightly and flicked his eyes her way. A small smiled played across his face. "If I was married to Mark, I'd have sex with fat fucking Bob too."

Kendal laughed. "Well, you're not. You're married to me, and I say you need to go. You need to get out of the house."

"I'm out of the house right now."

Kendal rolled her eyes and increased the pressure on the accelerator. This discussion could wait until later. First, she must get through the trip to Dangriga.

Finally reaching the highway, it was necessary to stop at the intersection and offer the two young Garifuna men a ride to Dangriga, because that's what they were waiting for and that's what you did in Belize. It was an easy, welcome task with Charlie there but not something she embraced when alone. They looked to be near twenty and locals, but they were unknown to her or Charlie. Kendal drove with quiet caution as Charlie chatted them up. They were from Dangriga, on the way back home from Placencia. They were both studying tourism at the university, but just as soon as they had enough money, they were off to the United States.

"Oh, yes," one man bragged. "It will be New York I go to first. I have family in Chicago, but I will go to New York."

"It's big and dirty and smelly," Kendal told them. "Stay here."

Both men laughed. "No, it's beautiful. The lights, the buildings, good parties, always something to do."

"And lots of beautiful women," injected the other.

"Well, you are right about that," agreed Charlie, and Kendal let the conversation go.

It always amazed her how many of the young Belizeans wanted to immigrate to the US. She'd read somewhere that there were as many Belizeans living in the States as there were living in Belize. She found it sad that the rich Garifuna culture seemed to be slipping away with the young.

Of the many cultures that defined Belize, the Garifuna was one that Kendal especially loved and admired. People created by man's inhumanity to man, by greed and circumstances, this culture, these people—descendants of Carib, Arawak, and African peoples—had survived all that time had thrown at them. Beginning with a shipwreck on the island of Saint Vincent, would-be African slaves, never reaching American soil, blended their genes, their knowledge, and their tenacity with the already-intermingled Venezuelan Caribs and island Arawaks—and the Garifuna were born. They lived in relative peace with the French colonists for years until the British came, sparking death and war. The victorious British forcibly removed what was left of the Garifuna people to Roatan, one of the Bay Islands off Honduras, where they eventually migrated to the mainland and colonized along the Caribbean coast. Now, two hundred years later, they were still struggling to keep their language, their history, their traditions—their place in the world.

Kendal wanted to remind these young men of this, to remind them what their parents and grandparents had surely taught them. But she drove and kept her mouth shut. Let them dream their dreams, and if they managed to make it to the US, then they could see for themselves what they had left behind.

They dropped their hitchhikers off with smiles and waves before they turned toward the airport. Kendal made it to the tiny runway in plenty of time for the flight. It would be a happy bride who walked down the aisle adorned with handmade custom jewelry all the way from Belize. It felt good to be relieved of her burden. Did her clients picture her as a dark-skinned, smiling Belizean, working out of a tiny shack by the sea, arduously hand-cutting and polishing the stone by the light of a flickering tiki torch while her hungry children played in the sand? Or did they know what she really was: a relatively rich, displaced expat from New Jersey? And which would be a prouder thing to wear upon your wrist?

Kendal found a parking space near the bank and turned to Charlie, who looked tired and hot. "You don't want to come in?" she asked him.

"I will if you really need me to." His hand came out and rested on her thigh. "But you need to know that it's you, not me, that gets you through each day."

She blinked hard at him and shook her head. Where was this coming from? What had he been stewing about while she was in Tropic Air? Since when did need and want become the same thing? All she'd wanted was a little company. "So you did not want to come?"

"No. That's not it at all. I wanted to come with you. I'll always want to be with you... but it's not always going to be possible. I won't always be here for you." She shook her head harder, and she felt his hand tighten on her leg. "You need to believe me when I say that you do this all on your own."

"You can just stop talking now."

"Each day you make it through," he continued. "Each success—it's always been you. I'm just along for the ride."

"I seriously don't want to talk about this."

"You can do this without me."

"Well, I don't want to," she nearly yelled, and he closed his eyes to her assault. Now she felt like a spoiled child who was being pushed from the nest—a child who wanted to fly, who was pissed off that she couldn't, and was hanging on to the twigs with all her strength.

"Kendal..."

"Fuck you." And she was out the door, slamming it shut and flouncing toward the bank.

Author Note: I always found it interesting and a little disturbing that so many of the Belizeans I've talked to want to move to the US. Wiki says there are over fifty thousand Belizeans living in the States, which is a lot considering we're talking about a country that only has a population of

about four hundred thousand. Is it a "the grass is always greener" phenom-enon? Is it "marketing" on the part of the United States? Is it financially motivated? Interestingly, many Belizeans immigrated in the 1940s, '50s, and '60s during the Great Migration of black southerners to the US Mid-west after World War II and after Hurricane Hattie hit Belize in 1961. Most settled in Chicago, where, due to chain migration ("My cousin lives there, so I'll go there too."), there still remains a large cultural community of Belizean expats.

Chapter 19: Calling up the Gods

Charlie sat back and sighed. Well, that hadn't gone as planned. He thought of the early days of their romance, the funny, quirky young girl with big blue eyes, stubborn and fragile at the same time. What had changed in the ten years he'd known her? Nothing and everything. He knew that she was frightened and lonely and angry with him—already feeling the loss of him. And now that he knew, without a doubt, what Aaron had become—it should have brought on his own anger. Although he couldn't quite put his finger on what he was feeling, it wasn't really anger. His concern for Kendal, which had been growing steadily over the last few months, was now stalled and eased by an irritating relief.

What he'd tried to tell her was true. What he'd needed her to know was that she would be okay without him—without anyone. She would have always been okay, even if he had not stepped out of that grocery store ten years ago and fallen in love. Sure, he let himself fall into the role of her protector; and, yes, it had been wrong in so many ways. But she was, even ten years ago, the strongest person he'd ever known. And this was what he'd tried to tell her and failed. But it was possible that it was *he* that needed to believe—to know—that she would be okay. Perhaps it was something she already knew—had always known.

The car was hot now, the sun having broken through the clouds. A faint breeze was doing little to move the stale odor of civilization that had permeated the car. He rolled the window down fully and tilted his head out, in reminiscence of his old hound dog, Freddy. Good old Freddy—floppy spotted ears, goofy drooling tongue, dying an old and crippled thing—dead now twenty years. He closed his eyes and sighed. The sounds of life—the traffic, the people walking by, the calls of friendly recognition and commerce, the happy and not-so-happy screeches of children—pushed through the quickly rising humidity.

He'd crossed the street, that very first time he'd seen her, and offered her a hand with the unruly and unreasonably large backpack she was toting. He could still see the look she'd given him, a soft mixture of amusement and skepticism, as she said dryly, "I've carried this thing all the way from Veracruz." She threw the pack, as gently as one could throw such a burden, and he caught it with minimum effort. "I'd say it's about time someone else took over." Then her laughter joined his, and the sound of her merriment was almost more than he could bear, causing him to nearly drop the thing. But he'd held on to all that she had thrown his way.

Now he opened his eyes, not to the sound of her laughter but to the sound of her opening the driver's side of the truck. She flung the deposit receipt his way, got in, slammed the door, and leaned her head back against the headrest. "I have a right to be angry," she stated.

"Yes. And so do I. But what, and who exactly, are you angry with? I don't think it should be me. It's not like I urged my body to betray me." He said this lightly and even managed a little laugh at the end. "It's not like I called up the gods and begged them to knock me down."

Kendal laughed as she gasped back a sob. "You did. You called them. I saw their number right next to the bed." She was crying now. "I hate you. All those long-distance charges."

He laughed, and he reached for her. "And don't be mad at me just because I worry about you. But I know you're going to be okay. I know it like I know that ice is cold—like I know how much you love me. And I think you know it too."

"I know no such thing," she sobbed in his arms. "I only know I hate you and don't want you to go."

Author Note: Is it torment or comfort to know that a loved one is dying? More time to prepare but fraught with possible complications of the heart.

Chapter 20: Rub-A-Dub-Dub

In the end, he went fishing. Not because he felt any differently about his companions but because the reasons not to go were so many fewer than the reasons to go. He could certainly handle Mark and Aaron. He'd spent most of his life dealing with people who did not thrill him personally: CEOs, government officials, other lawyers, his parents, his own daughters. Perhaps the only exception, pre-Belize, had been his first wife. That was the one skill he was good at. Not picking careers or socks that matched or which tie to wear or books to read or cars to buy—but women—he was good at picking women. When his wife had died a slow, insidious death... Well, he knew something about loss and being left behind. He knew about the loneliness and the isolation—the need for a warm and healthy body to ease you through the transition. He knew about anger and hatred, the feeling of betrayal, and watching someone die with grace. That was the true gift she had given him. Dying with grace. And that was the one gift, more than anything else, he wanted to leave with Kendal. So in the end, he went fishing.

The cold front of the previous day had blown out to sea, so the day dawned a lovely thing. They drove to the marina as the sun was just peeking over the sea. Kendal had packed food for three, and Aaron and Mark hauled two large coolers to the boat—one for the bait and all the fish that they were sure to catch; the other (if Mark had anything to do with it) was undoubtedly filled with beer. Aaron offered to captain the boat, but Charlie would be damned if he'd let that happen. He had no doubt that he could navigate these tricky waters better than Aaron could navigate getting out of his own bed. The engine complained briefly then fired into life. She'd been a good boat, purchased seven years ago after Charlie sold the sailboat.

Charlie eased the fishing boat from its slip at the marina while Aaron and Mark settled themselves and the gear. Mark fiddled with one of the rods as if he wasn't quite sure where to put the bait. He wore a stupid-looking cowboy hat, a two-day-old beard, aviator sunglasses, and an old, tattered gray Ohio State T-shirt. Charlie tried to feel some sort of compassion for the man, but somehow, it was easier for him to rest his eyes on Aaron, looking well-groomed and alert, than to linger on Mark's despair. Aaron's hair was pulled back in a neat ponytail that was slipped through his baseball cap. He wore a simple shirt, and his legs were covered in light hiking pants, and he sat quietly sipping on his coffee. Charlie watched as Aaron placed his dark sunglasses over his eyes and pulled the visor of his cap forward, masking the look of contriteness that Charlie both enjoyed and found insulting—as if there was even the slightest possibility of some sort of penance.

Charlie used his middle finger to push up his own sunglasses and shook his head at the absurdity of this little outing. But he eased his eyes off Aaron and onto the task at hand, physically negotiating the river and mentally negotiating the day.

They reached the mouth of the river where the waters argued with the sea, but the sea ultimately won, and the river was lost and forgotten. As they watched the momentary battle of waters, there was a sudden eruption, something slow and large, off the bow.

"What the hell is that?" asked Mark.

"Manatee," Aaron told him, and then Mark practically fell off the boat to get another view of the creature, but it was gone. Charlie chuckled softly and shook his head.

Aaron laughed and turned to Charlie. "Frank told me this morning that snook were biting at the river mouth."

Charlie nodded, brought the boat to a stop, and let it drift. He picked out two brightly colored lures from the tackle box and handed them to Aaron. "Use those ten-weight rods," he said. "I'm going to try this Seaducer, and we'll see what works."

Aaron attached the lures and handed a rod to Mark. "Have you ever cast this type of rig?" When he was answered by a blank stare, Aaron asked with a laugh, "Have you ever cast?"

"I fished in the 'Old and Tangy' once in Ohio," laughed Mark. "Caught an old shoe and a nice leather belt."

"Old and Tangy?"

"Our endearment in Columbus for the Olentangy River that runs through the city. It's not exactly clean but better than it used to be."

"So you've never caught a fish?" asked Charlie with disbelief. "Not even as a kid?"

Mark shrugged without apology. "My dad was a total geek. My mom—a librarian."

"Unbelievable," Charlie grumbled.

"Hey! Does the state fair count?" Mark smiled. "My third Ping-Pong ball went right into the little glass bowl."

Charlie laughed.

"What the fuck are you talking about?" asked Aaron.

"You know," Charlie said. "Those booths at the fairs where you throw the Ping-Pong balls at the fish bowls to win a goldfish."

Mark pointed at Charlie. "That's right. I named him Otto. From that book I read as a kid. Dr. Seuss, I think. I tried to feed him a lot of food so that he'd grow, just like in the story, but no swimming pool was ever needed." Mark shrugged. "He just died."

"Now you've totally lost me," said Aaron with a laugh.

"Dr. Seuss," Mark insisted. "Kids' books. The goldfish that gets bigger and bigger." Aaron shook his head incredulously, and Charlie chose not to get involved. If Dr. Seuss books did not make the top-seller list in South Africa and state fairs did not exist, it was none of his concern.

"So, anyways... let me show you how to use this thing without using your eye for bait," said Aaron as he went through the technical aspects of the rig.

Charlie cast his line with ease and watched as the lure sailed over the water. It hit inches from his intention and slipped just under the surface. He waited a moment and then reeled back with mild anticipation.

Aaron continued with his tutorial until Mark was casting respectably and then took up his own line. "You want to get as close to the mangroves as you can without getting yourself tangled. Snook usually hang out in the roots, and if they like what they see, they'll fly out and hit your line like lightening, so be ready," Aaron told Mark.

"Be ready for what exactly?" asked Mark with trepidation.

Charlie and Aaron both laughed. "To catch your first goddamn fish," said Charlie as he cast again, sending his lure to the edge of the mangroves. They were silent, the hiss of the lines and the soft plop as the bait hit the sea the only sounds they caused.

After about twenty minutes without a strike, and untangling Mark's line from the roots for the third time, Charlie started the boat and said, "Let's go on out to the cays."

Charlie swung around Sittee Point and headed out to sea. The sea remained calm, allowing him to push the throttle forward until they were almost effortlessly skimming along the ten or so miles to the first of the cays. The distant islands grew larger, and it wasn't long before individual palms could be appreciated. Charlie had to slow the boat to watch for patch reefs, some obvious as their brown arms reached above the surface, while others were lurking unseen, waiting to tear at the boat. The sun was bright, warming the air and bringing forth the beauty of the changing depths and the shifting ocean floor—dark greens, pale blues, azure, and turquoise. Charlie smiled. These waters dotted with cays—the splendid palm-covered white-sand islands off the coast of Belize—were, and had always been, the most amazing visual pleasure.

"It's as I remember it," said Mark with a sigh. "Cathy and I came out here from Placencia. To snorkel. It was a day like today, with the water like glass." He glanced from Charlie to Aaron and then away, back to the sea. "We were on our honeymoon."

"Yes. I think we knew that." Charlie shook his head mildly and then set his mind to getting them safely through the waters. "Why don't we try around this little patch reef?"

Aaron set the anchor. They baited the lines, and it was only a couple of casts—dropping the sinker to the bottom—before he and Aaron had caught the first of several snapper. "Make sure your line has hit the bottom. Drop until the line goes slack, then tighten just a bit," Charlie suggested to Mark, who was looking left out and abandoned.

"Like this?" he asked. He was looking at Charlie for approval when his hand jerked forward, and he nearly lost the rod. "Damn!" he said. "I think I got something."

"Yes, you do," agreed Charlie. The surface of the water split apart, and a huge silver fish leaped into the air. "Would you look at that," Charlie said in wonder.

"It's a fucking tarpon," whispered Aaron. "On a chunk of conch. Out here of all places. Un-fucking-believable."

"What the hell *is* that?" Mark exclaimed.

"It's your fish, you moron," laughed Aaron.

Charlie shook his head.

"Oh! Jesus!" said Mark, holding the rod with both hands, the line spinning out as the fish jumped again. "Someone hand me a beer!"

"Just let him have a little line. Grab the handle," said Charlie, feeling the excitement of the battle, thinking of his own fish tales—the bittersweetness of victories, the frustration of defeat. "Take it slow. You don't want him to break the line."

Mark heeded his advice, and it wasn't all that long before the fish was spent and Mark was able to bring it alongside the boat.

They studied the lovely silver creature, floating exhausted off the side of the boat, for a few moments before Aaron said, "That's one hell of a first fish. People spend hundreds of dollars to try to catch one of these fuckers, and you just go out and get one, like you knew what you were doing."

"I guess we'll have plenty of fish to go around for dinner," grinned Mark.

"No. It's a game fish. It's catch and release only," Charlie told him.

"Oh."

"Doesn't mean we can't get one hell of a good photo, though," said Aaron.

It took all three of them to get it out of the water and into Mark's hands so he could hold it up, the fish nearly as tall as Mark, and smile toward the camera. And when it was freed, back in the water and slowly swimming away, Mark reached into the cooler. "Anyone else ready for a beer?"

Charlie looked up to the sun. It was not quite ten. "It's a little too early for me," he stated. Aaron shook his head. Mark twisted off the top happily and took a long, noisy gulp.

When the sun was high in the sky, Charlie began to feel a little light-headed. Knowing his blood sugar level was dropping quickly, he eased the boat toward South Water Caye and brought the boat into the shallow waters off the white-sand beach. "You both go ashore and eat," he said. "I'm going to stay on the boat. Right here under the canopy."

As the two men made their way to the beach, Charlie settled in with the lovely sandwich Kendal had prepared. Good bread was something quite impossible to buy in Belize, so Kendal had learned, years ago, how to bake a crusty, hearty mix of grains. In between the thick slices of the bread, she'd placed thinly sliced layers of chicken and toma-toes, dark-green leaves of lettuce and sprigs of cilantro, and slivers of cu-

cumbers and sweet onions. And what made the sandwich truly divine was the addition of the perfect combination of mayo and Marie Sharp's hot sauce. He sighed with contentment and chewed.

Charlie took in the beauty that surrounded him—the beauty he'd almost come to take for granted—knowing that it might be the last time he took this image in, and he was suddenly glad that he'd come. How many people died never seeing a view such as this? And how often do you get to watch someone catch such a fish? His eyes went to Aaron and Mark, who were stretched out under a palm. Aaron was laughing, his head thrown slightly back at something Mark must have said. Charlie narrowed his eyes in thought, his lips pinching together in a tight frown. As much as he tried to hate the man, he just couldn't seem to get past the fact that Aaron was impossible to hate. The task was made all the more difficult because he had grown to love Aaron—to love him like a son. Charlie sighed, took another bite of the sandwich, and turned back to the sea.

Charlie loved a fresh snapper, cooked whole with just a hint of spice. But there was nothing like a grouper, cooked within moments of its death, the sweet white flakes melting on your tongue, and the knowledge that you had procured this pleasure with your own shrewdness, your own skill. This had been his goal, his desire for the day. So after a long leisurely lunch, they pulled away from the cay to try their luck, one more time, among the patch reefs. He chose his spot in the sea carefully and his bait with expertise. Then he turned his mind away from Aaron, away from Kendal, and turned to fishing.

Charlie set his line close to a nice little patch and let the bait sink.

Aaron sat near the bow, and Charlie watched as he cast his line with a soft hiss through the air.

"Thank you, Charlie," Mark said, "for bringing me out here." He and Aaron both turned their eyes to Mark. Mark was sitting on the middle bench of the boat and had not bothered to pick up his own rod. He was slurring his words ever so slightly. "I know it wasn't something you really wanted to do." And then Mark stopped awkwardly, glanced at Aaron, and added, "You know, with you not feeling so good. And you too, Aaron. Thanks. To both of you, for helping me catch my first real fish."

Charlie laughed, along with Aaron, and reached for his own beer. He was well into his second bottle now and feeling it. When was the last time he'd had more than one beer? His doctors had warned him about alcohol when he developed the diabetes. But what was the worst thing a few beers could do to him now? Kill him? He laughed again. "Thank you, Mark, for letting me see all this through the eyes of an Ohioan—like it's all brand new."

Mark laughed and brought his own beer up for a toast. "To Belize."

Charlie and Aaron leaned toward the center of the boat and clicked their bottles against Mark's.

"And to one big fucking fish," added Aaron, tilting back his bottle and taking in a long swallow.

"And to Kendal's wonderful lunch," added Mark.

"Man! That woman can cook!" exclaimed Aaron, who was apparently a little drunk himself. Charlie narrowed his eyes Aaron's way as Aaron said, "Remember that fucking shark she cooked for us, Charlie? It was fucking awesome." Then Aaron turned back to his fishing line—his smile turning soft and wistful.

"Why is it," demanded Charlie, each word increasing with anger, "that every other word out of your mouth is 'fuck' or 'fucking'?"

Aaron's smile evaporated. He turned back toward Charlie. "I don't know."

"Well, it's just absurd. Or should it be *fucking* absurd?"

Aaron titled his head down and rubbed at his forehead. "Sorry." Then he looked up at Charlie, a laugh escaping from his mouth. "I mean... I'm fucking sorry!"

Charlie stared at Aaron, his face constricting to a deep frown.

"Cathy's a great cook."

Charlie forced his eyes off Aaron. "What?" he said with disbelief.

"Cathy," Mark said sadly. "She's a great cook. Like Kendal."

Aaron was holding his stomach with laughter, and Mark was swaying with the boat and staring at his beer despondently. Charlie closed his eyes and tried to check his temper. "This isn't funny," he all but yelled. "What the hell is so funny?"

"What's so funny?" cried Aaron through his laughter. He spread his arms out in a wide sweep. "This is what's so funny! Here we are, the three of us, out here in this fucking boat. You wanting to kill me and Mark wanting to kill himself and me... Well, I don't even know why I'm here! That's what's so fucking funny!"

Charlie glared at Aaron.

"Cathy made these really incredible ribs—all slathered in sauce..."

Charlie's line suddenly snapped tight, bending the pole, and he automatically laid his rod against the rail of the boat and started reeling in as fast as he could. "No, you don't," he said. "You're not going anywhere."

Aaron stopped laughing and leaned over Mark toward Charlie until he was peering into the crystal-clear water. "There he is. Damn, he's a big one."

Charlie could see him, too, the large, dark grouper struggling against the line, and already, his arms were starting to ache.

"Let me help you."

Charlie flashed Aaron a look. "Absolutely not." He stopped winding in and just pulled against the drag. He'd used his pliers earlier and tightened down the drag as tight as it would go, and even this fish wasn't going to be able to break this line. The anchor line was tight, the boat secure—he could wait.

Aaron sat back away from Charlie and sipped his beer. Mark leaned over the boat and watched the fish. Charlie felt the sweat break out on his forehead, but he was unable to wipe it away for fear of losing his hold, so it trickled down around his eyes and onto his cheeks. He wiped at his face with the sleeves on his shoulders and shifted a bit on the bench. His hands started to cramp, so he hooked the reel between his knees and relaxed his grip just enough to ease the pain.

Aaron's empty beer clanked against the bottom of the boat as he set it down, the ice rattling as he reached for two more. He handed one to Mark.

Mark twisted off the top of the new beer and tapped Charlie gently on the arm with the end of the bottle. "Remember that book?" he asked. "*The Old Man and the Sea*?"

"Fuck you," Charlie managed to get out, and Aaron laughed.

"It was one of Cathy's favorite stories."

Aaron shoved Mark hard in the back, pushing him slightly into Charlie. "Would you shut the fuck up about Cathy?"

"But I love her. Almost nine years. We've been married almost nine years. How could she have done this to me? To our kids? God, I miss my kids..."

Charlie shook his head. He could feel the fish starting to tire. "Would you look at what you're doing to yourself?" He shot the words at Mark through his ragged breathing. "No woman is worth that."

"Not even Kendal?" challenged Mark.

"No. Not even Kendal," Charlie answered. He began to turn the handle, and the fish fought back, but slowly, its heavy body rose toward the boat.

Aaron readied the net when the fish was breaching the surface. Once the fish was secure, Charlie was able to relax his hold.

"This is one big old guy," Aaron said as they took in the large black grouper eyeing them with his tiny round eyes, his comically large mouth turned down in a perpetual frown. He was nearly four feet long, his gill flaps pumping with fatigue.

"He's nearly as long and a lot heavier than mine," said Mark. "How'd you manage to pull him in?"

Charlie didn't answer, his eyes fixed on the old fish.

Aaron said, "Grouper like to grab the bait and run back into the coral. Then you're screwed. Keeping him out of the coral, that's the key. Then it's just a matter of waiting him out. Hanging in there until the fish is spent. Good equipment, stamina, and patience—you'll always win in the end."

Charlie brought his hand to his forehead and rubbed it softly. "Let him go," he said without looking toward Aaron.

"What?"

Charlie set down the rod and turned away from the men—away from the fish. "Unhook him and let him go."

"But I thought you really wanted to eat some grouper tonight. This fish will give you grouper for a month."

Charlie didn't answer.

"Help me, will you?" Aaron asked Mark.

Charlie closed his eyes as the two men unhooked the fish. There was a sharp slap, the sudden spray of water, and the fish was gone.

Author Note: I believe this was my favorite chapter to write. Not only did I have the perfect venue to get these three men together, but I had the opportunity to learn. I love doing research and contacted my friend Wayne to ask him about fishing in the waters of Belize. He used to own the house next to ours in Hopkins, and there wasn't a day that went by that I didn't see him either fishing in the sea or the river or the canal. I grew up fishing in Lake Murray in South Carolina, so catching bass and brim was about the extent of my repertoire. While Google is a wonderful source of knowledge, there's nothing like getting direct info from an expert. Thanks, Wayne!

Chapter 21: Fish Stories

The three men sat at the table near the beach and watched as the sky turned toward night. They were still drinking, but slower now, and enjoying the chips and salsa Kendal had provided. The good smells of fish cooking were wafting down from the grill on the veranda, and it was just possible to hear Kendal as she sang while she cooked. Charlie was feeling the weight of the day, fatigue settling around him. Aaron and Mark seemed to be hitting their stride, all of the earlier tension gone as the two men laughed and joked about nonsense. He closed his eyes, and he sighed. He could not deny that it had, overall, been a good day—the kind of day he remembered from before he got sick—the kind of day that defined his life in Belize. So there was a smile on his face as he saw Kendal come down the stairs, her long legs looking beautiful in the setting sun, carrying the large platter of fish and vegetables.

"Wow. Thank you for cooking for us," he said as she set the platter on the table.

"Hey, you men worked hard—all that hunting. I gathered. I cooked. It is as it should be." She went to the cooler and took out a beer. "Anyone else?"

Charlie took inventory of the bottles on the table and said, "No, we're good." But his gaze lingered on her—a question, a concern in his look. He knew this would be her third beer, and alcohol was something she normally avoided. He raised his eyebrows ever so slightly, and she challenged him with a look of her own. Well, okay, then.

"My God, this looks good," slurred Mark. "I'm starved. I could eat that entire grouper you caught, Charlie."

"Grouper?" Kendal asked.

Aaron answered. "We let him go. He looked like he still had some things to get done, you know?"

Kendal smiled as she placed a fish on each plate. "I'm glad. Grouper numbers are dropping. Some species are seriously in trouble. And besides, these snapper you guys caught are all we need."

The table grew quiet as they concentrated on the delicacy of the food, closing their eyes to the slight evening breeze that pushed aside the heat of the day. A dog barked somewhere in the village and was answered by another and then another. They ate until their stomachs were uncomfortable, until all the fish was gone, until the sky was dark and all that lit the night were the tiny citronella candles that flickered in the breeze.

"Tell me your fish stories."

Charlie opened his eyes, and Kendal was looking at him.

"There must be fish stories." Her eyes left Charlie's and shifted to Mark's and then to Aaron's.

"Oh my god. What a great day," exclaimed Mark. "It's so amazing out there."

"Mark caught his very first fish," Aaron told her. "All by himself."

"My little boy," Kendal swooned. "He's growing up!"

"It was a big one too!" grinned Mark. "A tarpin."

"Tarpon," Aaron laughed.

"Whatever. It was huge, almost as big as I am."

"Wow."

"It was incredible. Better than sex."

Aaron and Kendal laughed. "What kind of sex have you been having?" asked Kendal.

"Well... none. But as I recall it, the fish was better."

They all laughed.

Kendal reached out and squeezed Mark's arm. "That, my boy, needs to change. We need to get you laid. I haven't forgotten. I'm still looking."

"Surely, there must be someone," said Aaron. "She only has to be as good as a fish."

Kendal laughed. "Oh, I think she ought to be at least a little better."

"Hey. Whatever," said Mark.

Kendal's head went back as she laughed, the glow of candlelight painting her face, her lovely teeth reflecting the light.

Charlie took his empty bottle of beer and forced it, lip down, into the sand until all that was visible was the butt end. He turned toward Mark, who looked glassy-eyed as he watched her laugh, a smitten drunk smile on his face. His gaze shifted to Aaron, who was grasping his beer with two hands and leaning toward the laughter. Charlie leaned back.

"You know," he said loudly, stopping the laughter and turning all eyes his way. "We're all just one big happy family here, aren't we?" He was aware that his words were slurred and louder than necessary. His gaze fell on Kendal. "Really, my darling Kendal, you ought to just fuck Mark too. That would really make it cozy."

There was a beat of silence as he watched Kendal's mouth drop open.

"Jesus fuck, Charlie!" said Aaron.

Kendal was up and then gone, the slap of her feet against the concrete steps decreasing in volume until all that could be heard was the sigh of the sea.

Charlie closed his eyes with a soft moan and brought his hand up in support of his head. "I'd say 'Jesus fuck' is about right," he mumbled. "Hand me another beer, will you?"

And Aaron did.

He woke up in his leather chair, and she was staring at him. He shifted and rubbed at his face as if it were a problem.

"How long have you known?" she asked.

He must have fallen asleep here, unable to make it as far as the bedroom. He swallowed away the dryness of his sleep and cleared his throat. He looked at her—perched in her chair, her long legs tucked beneath her, a steaming cup of coffee in her hand, her eyes like pale-blue moons. He saw his own cup of coffee waiting for him, so he reached for it and tasted the pleasure of the bitterness.

"A couple days," he finally managed.

She nodded her head slowly. "It was a hell of a way to let me know you knew."

"Yes." He sighed. "It was unintentional."

"But, perhaps, deserved."

"No."

"And how are you?"

He shook his head in confusion. "How are you?"

"Sad."

Yes, that was it... not true anger, nor jealousy, certainly not disbelief. But just plain sadness. He nodded in agreement, and then she stood up, teased his face with the tips of her fingers, and disappeared into her studio.

Author Note: I'm not much of a fisherman, but I do have a fish story. Once, we were out at the cays, fishing in our new panga with a local Garifuna fishing guide named Bert. We had bought the boat used. Although it had seen better days, it felt new to us. The very first fish someone caught was a big barracuda. Before I knew what was happening, the fish was flopping around on the boat deck, his impressive set of teeth snapping. Bert shouted in his heavy accent for me to hand him the club. The club? I started searching under the seats, and sure enough, the boat had come equipped

with a big wooden stick. Caught up in the moment, I handed him the club. A few bashes on this poor fishy's head, and blood was flying all over our deck, all over our seats, and all over us! Gruesome for sure, but the look of unabashed joy that took over Bert's face in response to the look on mine was priceless and worth the job of having to clean the boat. "Fish murderer," I called him, and he laughed with glee.

Chapter 22: Hugging the Octopus

It was after lunchtime before she emerged from her studio and went to the beach. She swam in the warm, soft waves until her arms ached and her legs felt like jelly. She kicked her way past Yugadah and saw Mark sitting under a palm, glumly sipping coffee. She offered him a quick wave of her hand; but he did not seem to want to talk any more than she did, and she was happy to leave it at a wave.

Again, she felt the mild anger toward Charlie and kicked a little harder. The way he'd used Mark like a pawn. Mark, who'd been sucked innocently and unwittingly into their little drama. Kendal stopped swimming and sank under the waves—this little drama of her own creation...

When she felt she could no longer swim without the risk of drowning, she sat in the surf in front of her house, the waves gently slapping at her thighs, and watched the dive boat come in. It wasn't long before he made it up the beach and joined her in the surf, sitting close and leaning back with fatigue.

She looked at his face—still red and creased with the lines of the diving mask—wrinkles of concern on his forehead, the white crust of salt already forming around his mouth.

She fought the urge to lick at the salt and said, "Hard dive?"

"Alcohol and nitrogen, a bad mix." He leaned closer, and his hand touched hers, the foaming sea slipping around their fingers. "How are you? Are you okay?"

"Charlie's on the veranda."

Aaron turned toward the house and waved then leaned back her way. "I don't care. What he did to you last night was cruel."

"What we're doing is crueler."

He turned to the ocean and sighed. She closed her eyes and listened to the song of the sea and felt his fingers close upon her hand.

"I've got a dive scheduled for tonight. Come with us."

She felt the weight of his request—as if her answer would set all future answers.

She thought of all the tiny shrimp eyes, crazy pairs of headlights glowing against the coral. Surrounded by watery darkness, one's only view of this wet world was the flashlight beam. It was scary and exhilarating at the same time, never knowing what might show up in the shaft of light... a beautiful iridescent octopus slipping over the rocks; the amazing colors of coral polyps waving gently from their homes; a sleeping grouper turning away from the light like a grumpy old man; a lobster with claws the size of melons. Clicking off all the lights and waving at the water until a magnificent show of luminescence teased her eyes; shining her light at only Aaron as he floated above her and feeling like they were the only two souls on earth—which they weren't.

"I can't," she told him. She felt Aaron's hand slipping away, the weight of her body easing into the sand as a wave retreated to the sea.

It had hit her, falling-rock fast. One moment, she'd had everything under control, and the next moment, it was sneaking up on her and banging at her very core. It didn't have a name or a face, but it was more real than anything she'd ever felt, and she felt it like a wet terror. And there was nowhere to run that didn't bring it right along.

It had been in chemistry class, her senior year of college, when it became no longer possible to hide the terror from her fellow students. The danger, so great that it was her duty to warn people—to prepare. Her hands grasping Melissa Kramer's arm as she pleaded, "You need to understand the danger that you're—" Melissa stepping back and grabbing the nearest beaker as if to launch it at her. Falling to her knees and grasping at Tyler Steinman's calves. "Surely you see it, Tyler? Please, you need to understand!" Tyler pulling away in horror; she could still see the look on his face. He hadn't understood—hadn't understood at all.

Then it became a desperate thing, the crushing panic, the inability to get the words to her tongue, then the need to get away—to save herself. But even as she tried to run, the terror crashing around her, the people wouldn't let her be—captured like a dying moth. All she wanted was to get away, but she was a withering, fluttering captive creature, and they forced her to where she would never choose to be. The harsh lights, the restriction of her body, the panic in her parents' eyes, the inhumanity. But what exactly was her crime to humanity? It must be fitting to the punishment. Surely, she was deserving of this awful thing—the needles, the straps, the cruel words—so that in the end, the crime fit the punishment, and she'd become all that they thought her to be.

She was handed the word, given the label, offered no real reprieve, no permanent repair. The word, an ugly word, as misunderstood as it was ugly. Not a splitting of one's personality but a shattering of thought, a bombardment of sensation, an overwhelming fear of standing still and of progressing forward—a fear of life, of death... of words such as "schizophrenia."

When she was finally free and able to feel the sun on her face and the grass between her toes, there was hardly anything left of her to feel. It didn't help that her parents held her as if she would break and then tiptoed around the problem as if there wasn't a problem. If she brushed her hair, she was greeted with great patronizing enthusiasm, but if she talked about returning to school, she was shut down like a child—the expectations so low that it was hard to rise to greet the day. The pressure of no pressure was too much to bear.

She'd wanted to be a scientist, to unravel all the mysteries, to work in a room full of long, straight tubes of glass, of air spinning with ideas, and to know that she had some sort of understanding, some sort of control. But it was true. The core was gone. Shaken. Shattered. Long, straight tubes of glass were now just too straight. Words danced before her eyes, the printer told her all its secrets, the lullaby of the teakettle made her want to cry. Yes, there were days when brushing her hair was her only accomplishment. When she ventured into the world, there wasn't a face that didn't turn her way, that didn't cast judgment, not a word that didn't sail to her ears, not a soul that didn't want to see her dead—making her gulp down panic and scurry back home. But to be alone with the teakettle, the secrets of the printer, with the tiptoeing of her parents—with her failure...

With time, they came to understand. And if they did not embrace her decision, they did not pull it from her grasp, so she boarded the plane to Mexico, a large green backpack slung over her shoulders, her hair cut short and choppy from that argument she'd had with those scissors. It was a simple getaway to practice her Spanish, to gather sanity around her in a place where no one knew that she was gathering. She could return stronger, better, and able to know that she could walk upon the earth with some sort of understanding of where her feet were heading.

To practice Spanish with the seagulls, laugh with the waves, to knit together that which was scattered, to feel cohesiveness—this was what she sought in the warmth, in the sun, in the sea the color of skies. And she sensed it, breathed in the calmness and felt once again—with tentative hope—the joy of life. It was in a little market, on the side street of Medellin—with the sun blasting down on her back, with Mexican children grasping at her hips, reaching toward her blond tufts of hair—that she'd studied, like a child, the intricate patterns of pretty stone laid into the silver. She looked with wonder at the dark, round, smiling face of acceptance telling her in slow and careful Spanish that she had created the jewelry. Kendal reached for the bracelet, her hands lingering on the cool, soft folds of the woman's hand, and asked her, in shaking, pleading Spanish, if she could be taught to do such a thing—to realign tiny shattered pieces of stone into something truly beautiful.

The return ticket was never used, and there was nothing her parents could say or do to force her from her stones. When she'd learned all that she could learn from Rosa, she hugged her to her chest until they were both wet with tears, slung her large pack across her shoulders, and started walking toward the south, along the sea. There was no agenda, no destination. She simply walked, following the song of her sandals as they met, with each step, the dusty warmth of the earth.

It was with relief that she threw the pack Charlie's way and watched with pleasure as his eyes lit up to the task. She'd allowed him to carry the weight, not because it was more than she could handle but because it felt good to share the task of living. He made it easy to share, with his warmth, his calmness, never judging or struggling when she wrapped her tentacles of need about him; and he was never hurt from the sudden spray of inky darkness as she withdrew back into her cave of solitude. So she'd carved out a life of stones and of love, of novels on Friday nights, of waterfalls and drops into the deepness of the sea. And this life had pushed away the dark voices of her soul and allowed her to be both at peace and a piece of something which was beautiful.

And it was beauty she turned from and met as she turned Aaron's way.

Kendal followed Aaron's fingers in the sand until they were part of hers and turned her eyes to his and did not move to distract the tears that rolled down her cheeks. "That beautiful octopus that lives in that rocky crevice, give her a kiss for me, will you?"

Author Note: Mental illness is something I've touched on in all my previous novels. Illnesses such as schizophrenia, bipolar disorder, major depression, borderline personality, and obsessive-compulsive disorder affect one in five people. One out of four families have a member dealing directly with

these illnesses. That's a lot of people and a topic that historically has been avoided in fiction. The subject of serious mental illness remains relatively taboo and shrouded in shame, causing many who are suffering to avoid seeking help when there are many successful treatment options. We need to open up the discussion one story at a time!

Chapter 23: Swimming in the Dark

Charlie felt every day of his sixty-four years as he watched Kendal and Aaron from the veranda. In his mind, he'd walked with firm determination to the beach and joined them in the sand. "Well, good afternoon, Aaron," he'd say as he sat near his wife. He'd put a hand on her thigh and lean across her body and say, "And how was your dive, you bastard?"

He'd hit a man once. His hands ached with pleasure at the thought. He bit the inside of his lip until he tasted blood and looked down at his hands, which were tight, pathetic balls of knobby knuckles and blotched skin, and felt his anger slip away into despair.

Aaron passed on a beer as he joined Mark at King Kassava's. He told Mark he was simply interested in getting some food into his body before his night dive; but in Mark's professional opinion, Aaron looked like a beer might do him some good. Mark noted the weary sigh that pushed its way from Aaron's mouth as he sat down, and he missed the bubbling happiness he'd grown to depend on, the happy *hakuna matata* that had, in his mind, defined his new friend. And if they should both fall into deep despair—well, what would happen then? What would happen to him? Who would allow him to see his own stupidity?

"Hey! Why don't you take me on that dive of yours? Swim around in the dark." Which made Aaron laugh, just as he'd planned. "Really! It would be so cool!"

"You've never fucking dove in your life."

"I've snorkeled. Same thing, sans tank."

Aaron's face crinkled into amusement. "Yeah... okay. Like Valium and Viagra are the same."

"Yeah." Mark frowned. "I mixed those up once. Nobody was very happy."

Now Aaron's laugh turned into something deep, and they both laughed as if it were contagious. When Aaron's laughter faded away, he turned his attention to the TV over the bar until Frank brought his food. He lifted a forkful of beans into his mouth without pleasure and chewed as he gazed toward the street, absently watching the movement of the village.

Mark had about as much interest in throwing himself underwater with metal tanks strapped to his back as he had of slowly pulling off the nail of his right big toe. After all, he'd seen during the fishing trip, with his own two eyes, what sort of creatures lurked there. But he tapped his beer bottle gently on the table and said, "You know... learning to dive would be kinda cool."

Aaron's eyes turned from the street to Mark. "You really want me to teach you to dive?" He laughed. "I'll teach you. In the daylight. Starting in the pool. Tomorrow if you like. It would be a hoot to see you try to breathe underwater. Of course," Aaron continued, "there's a lot more involved than the technical aspects. Buoyancy, safety stuff, pressure, volume, calculating dive times... I could get you a manual. It'll give you something to do other than whatever it is you do all day." His voice drifted off, and his thoughts appeared to turn away from diving as he tapped his fingers nervously on the table and stared back at the television over the bar.

"You know," said Mark. "I read about it once but never quite got the whole pressure, volume, and density thing."

Aaron turned from the TV. "Are you seriously interested in diving?"

Mark shrugged a "Why not?" and Aaron began to talk. As he talked, his mood lifted, until he was talking with his standard rapid speech.

As Mark sat and listened to him explaining the basic relationship between pressure, volume, and density, he considered, as he toyed with his warming beer: just how necessary was the nail on his right big toe?

Kendal emerged from her studio as the sun was setting, meeting Charlie's eyes with mutual pain as he looked up from the book he was reading in his leather chair. He looked away, and she walked across the room to the kitchen. She removed her largest pot and began to fill it with water. Pasta was all she felt capable of preparing—maybe a carbonara with those fresh eggs Theresa had given her. A fresh salad from what they had purchased at the market. And then even that seemed overwhelming. She watched as the water reached the lip, cascaded down the sides of the pan, and disappeared into the drain; and then Charlie was there, shutting off the water and taking her into his arms.

"We can do this. We can do this together, just as we always have. This isn't so big, this thing with Aaron. I'm not a child. I see how things are. I love him too."

He whispered these words into her ear as he pressed her head into his chest, and she felt his fragility, smelled his dying old-man odor, and wondered if she'd ever loved him the way that she should have loved him—if she'd ever given him anything close to what he'd given her. And she felt, like a hot heavy oil, the reality that she resented him—begrudged him his very existence.

"Why? Why do you love me?" she pleaded.

"Oh, Kendal. How could I not? You... You are life. Your laughter, your smile, your crazy hair..." His fingers moved among the ropes of her hair until they found their way to her neck and then around to her chin, where he used them to lift her face to his. She closed her eyes to his kiss and then relaxed into the softness, into the movement of his lips against hers, and was rewarded by the flood of memories. Then she knew, without a doubt, as she wrapped her arms around him, that she did and had always loved him.

Author Note: Up until now, Mark has been a bit of a putz, but in this scene at the bar, there just may be hope for him!

Chapter 24: Don't Call Me Moron

Mark woke up early to the sound of rain beating like thunder above his head and smiled at his reprieve. There was no way Aaron would get him in a pool, strapped to some flimsy breathing device, in this kind of weather. He was about to slip back into sleep when, quite suddenly, he wondered what the date was. He knew, or was pretty sure, it was Thursday, but what was the date? He'd stepped on the plane November 25, the Saturday after Thanksgiving; of that he was certain. But he really had no idea how long he'd been here. Had it been two weeks? More? Was it nearly Christmas?

He sat up abruptly and had to clasp his head between his hands to stop the spinning. He closed his eyes to the sensation and could see, as if they were in the very room, last Christmas. Tracey ripping open the wrapper from that silly stuffed talking bear she wanted like she never wanted anything else; and Missy, her hair a tangled mess from sleep, her eyes shining in the Christmas-tree lights, playing with some tiny plastic doll with what seemed like hundreds of miniscule plastic dresses and shoes and hats, different styles and colors of hair. He heard their laughter, saw their little legs splayed out on the floor, covered in the goofy pink-footed pajamas his mother had given them. Saw the piles of ripped paper scattered across the floor, the unwrapped and still-to-be-unveiled gifts...

And he saw Cathy. Wrapped in her old, fuzzy green robe—the one with all the snags, the one with the hem ripped out on the bottom so that it was not even up to Goodwill standards. She was sitting across the room on the couch, her eyes alight as she watched her children. But her mind... What was on her mind? Him? Their marriage? Fat fucking Bob? And why was she across the room?

Then he had the vague memory of his eyes finding his wife on the couch that Christmas morning; and instead of the warm glow of love, a fleeting thought had skipped through his mind: she didn't look quite as good as she had when they'd married—a few extra pounds, that new haircut he didn't love, an older, slightly pasty face...

He pushed his hands through his hair and looked out to the churning gray sea. What kind of man was he to think such thoughts on Christmas—or any time, for that matter? As if the years had only taken from Cathy and left him still in his early twenties. He had, in some basic way, failed. He could see that now. Failed her, his marriage, his children. Should he have joined her on the couch? Refused to allow her thoughts of anyone but him? Bought her a new robe? Had he left her before he'd even left—leaving her so alone that even fat fucking Bob looked good?

He rose from the bed and dressed quickly, stepping out into the driving rain. He was soaked by the time he made it down the stairs and to the front of Yugadah. He tried the door, but it was locked.

"Cordelia, are you there?"

The only answer was the beating rain against the roof. He pressed his head against the window and could just make out the red and blue of the Belizean flag, which hung above the black, white, and yellow bands of the Garifuna flag—and to the right, the calendar he remembered was there. It wasn't possible, from this distance, to resolve the numbers within the small squares. He looked up and down the street, which was empty at this hour, as it was too early for the children to be making their way to school in their little yellow-and-brown uniforms. Today, they'd be twirling brightly colored umbrellas, the different colors bouncing along as all the little feet splashed their way up the street.

It was only a short walk to Aaron's place. He knocked on the old wooden door, which was not much more than three thin planks boarded together. When he received no answer, he knocked again and tried the door, which, as he suspected, was open. "Aaron?"

"Fuck, Mark. What do you want?" His voice was groggy with sleep.

"What's the date? I know it's Thursday, but what's the date?"

Mark stepped out of the rain and into the room. He could see Aaron in the gloom of the small room, stretched out across his bed, a thin sheet wrapped around his legs. The space was slightly larger than his, with a makeshift closet in one corner, the clothes hanging on a metal rod suspended from the ceiling, and a series of wooden pegs banged into the wall. There was no Sheetrock, so the interior walls were unfinished, unpainted wood. Aaron had taken advantage of the occasional nail banged in from the outside to hang up his extra things, decorating his walls with baseball caps, pairs of pants, T-shirts, damp socks, towels, and dive masks. Other than the bed, the only furniture was a small eating table and two wooden chairs. In the corner, opposite the bed, stood a neat but scary stack of appliances—a tiny refrigerator, which supported a microwave, which supported a toaster oven, which supported a coffeepot. The free area of the refrigerator top was occupied by a smattering of the most basic of eating utensils, which shook along with the coffeepot as Mark made his way across the room.

"I don't know what the date is." Aaron sat up in his bed and rubbed his eyes. "Shit. The tenth? Eleventh? I don't know." Aaron untangled the sheet from around his legs and stretched his arms over his head and yawned.

"But when is Christmas?"

"The twenty-fifth, you moron." His arms came down, and he scratched at his chest. "It's always the twenty-fifth."

"Don't call me a moron, asshole. I know it's the twenty-fifth, but how much time do I have before Christmas?"

"You're dripping all over my fucking floor."

Mark had stopped pretty much in the middle of the room, and he surveyed the items on the walls. "Don't you have a calendar somewhere in this place?"

"And why, exactly, would I need a calendar?" Aaron swung his feet from the bed and reached for the dirty pair of sweats wadded on the floor. "I guess I won't be going back to sleep." He yawned again. "Over there. On the table. Check my cell phone. That'll give you the date."

Of course. Mark had turned his off, as it didn't seem to work in Belize. He went to the table and flipped open Aaron's phone. Thursday, December 10. Two weeks. He sat down on one of the old wooden chairs and flipped the phone shut, closing his hand around the piece of technology as he rested his head in his hands. He studied the pattern of the drips of water he'd left on the wide planks of flooring. He couldn't even imagine a Christmas without his family—his girls. Once the gifts were unwrapped and they'd consumed a breakfast of greasy sausages and fat, crispy waffles—sticky and dripping with real maple syrup—they'd pile into the car and make the quick trip across town to Mark's parents' house. Cathy was an only child, so her parents would come, plus his brother, his sister, their families, all the kids—a madhouse of family friction and fun.

Mark was the youngest of his siblings, a midlife "whoops" baby who'd been horribly spoiled and loved, dressed up and shown around by his older sister like a living doll. Even now, she fawned over him, coddled him. His brother, the oldest of the three, had been Mark's hero growing up, and now he was a friend—a true friend, unlike fat fucking Bob. And his parents, they weren't young anymore. How many more Christmases would there be before someone was missing? It would break all their hearts, what Cathy had done. What had Cathy told them? Did they even know that he was gone? Did they all wonder if he was even still alive?

"So you'll be leaving us soon?" asked Aaron, who'd slipped on his sweats and was watching him from his place at the foot of his bed.

Mark looked up at Aaron and shook his head with uncertainty. "You know, I never even told her where I was going? Didn't really even know myself until I got to the airport. Oh, man, how long have I been drunk?"

Aaron laughed. "Two weeks, more or less. I recall a few moments of partial sobriety."

"Oh, you mean the times when I was puking from a hangover?"

Aaron laughed again and grew quiet as he looked gently at Mark and waited.

Mark ran his fingers through his hair and sighed. "If I wanted to, say, call the States, how exactly would I do that? Are there phone booths here in Hopkins?"

"Right there. In your hand. Just dial zero zero one first."

Mark opened his hand and stared at the phone and then set it back down on the table. "Well, now's not a good time. They're getting ready for school, for work. Maybe later. Tonight." He grinned softly at Aaron. "Maybe after a few beers."

Aaron met his grin. "Sure. Anytime. Use it whenever you want."

"I'll pay you. I'll pay you for the call."

"Don't be a fuckhead. It costs almost nothing." Aaron looked out the wooden slats of his one and only window and sighed. "We won't go out in this sort of weather. Too rough." Aaron got up and made his way to the coffeepot. "I've got some things to do at the dive shop, but if you come by... say about eleven thirty, we could get started."

Mark looked up with alarm. "Get started?"

"Sure." He opened the tiny refrigerator, causing the whole ensemble to shift and the coffeepot to teeter, and removed a bag of coffee grounds. "You're gonna call Cathy. Work everything out. Kissy-kissy, all that shit. We don't have a lot of time to get your open-water dive in. Thought we'd go out to the reef. Drop down the wall. Just eighty, maybe a hundred feet."

The words "open water" immediately brought to mind that awful movie Cathy had rented. Mark could see the final scene—a lone diving vest floating on the water—all that was left of the divers after two hours of movie misery. Then there was that cute little fish movie his girls loved... What the hell was it called? *Finding Nemo*, that was it. *Never, never go beyond the wall, little Nemo.* He knew exactly how it would go down... half a dozen hungry sharks, him floating helplessly upon the waves, too burdened by dive gear to get away... Aaron, safe on the boat, laughing like a fool while he yelled Mark's way, "Don't worry, they won't eat much!"

Mark watched Aaron fill the pot from the large jug of water and measure out the grounds. "You know, Aaron..." He chose his words carefully. "It's really nice of you to offer to help me get certified, get me started in the pool and all, but I don't want you using your free time working. Hell, you dive enough as it is. Besides, it's raining."

"Yeah. It would be a real shame to get wet while you're in the pool." Aaron flipped the pot on. It immediately gurgled into life, threatening to leap from its perch, before settling into brewing. Aaron turned his attention away from the coffeepot and onto Mark. "There's the bookwork to do. A lot. I mean, a fucking shitload of safety things I need to go over with you. You can get into a whole pile of trouble out there if you don't know what you're doing." Aaron picked up a coffee mug from the top of the refrigerator and blew out the dust from its interior. "Equipment failure, unhappy encounters with wildlife, knowing how to help your dive buddy if they get into trouble, the bends, nitrogen poisoning..." He blew into a second mug. Unsatisfied, he flipped it upside down and shook its contents toward the floor. Mark watched a small buglike object fall from the mug and onto the floor. "I could go on and on." He stopped talking and peered at Mark expectantly. When Mark didn't say anything right away, Aaron broke into a wide grin. "You're scared shitless, aren't you?" Mark shrugged sheepishly, and

Aaron's laughter filled the room. "I'm just messing with you. Don't you think I know you'd rather step in front of a bus than dive?"

Mark laughed with relief. "Buses. A lot faster than sharks."

Aaron's laughter continued. "Coffee?"

"That'd be great."

Author Note: And there you have it; Mark is finally starting to get it! I like the way his relationship with Aaron is developing. I hope you do too.

Chapter 25: Roots and Camaraderie

"**I** just don't know what I'm going to do with that man!" Theresa exclaimed. "There may be parts of him I'd miss, but let me tell you, that thing that sits on his shoulders—it's packed full of shit."

Kendal's laughter mixed with that of her companions. Theresa was one of the older women in the community who was still active in its politics. She was the one who people went to if there was an illness or a ceremony to organize or a man that wasn't treating his wife well. She was the one who moved the men to work or the children to behave. She was the go-between when there was a problem with the police and one of the tourists or if one of the local developers got out of line. If a dog died in the middle of the road and no one bothered to remove its bloated body, she was the one who insisted the thing be dealt with and buried. She was one of the few women in the village who still made the cassava bread and did not buy the imported bread from Honduras. And today, she'd decided, was the day the cassava should be processed.

They sat in a semicircle of chairs, which surrounded the pile of roots the men had trucked in from the farmland outside the village. The open structure, which was attached to the back of Yugadah Restaurant, was large enough to keep the women dry, their sweaters and light coats enough to keep them warm. Theresa reached into the pile of brown roots poured onto the sandy floor, a strand of gray-streaked hair falling free from the bright-colored scarf wrapped around her head, and extracted a fresh, unpeeled cassava tuber. She held up the particularly suggestive root, upright and stiff, for all the women to see. "It's a shame

God chose to attach such a lovely thing as this to something as lowly as a man."

The women cocked their heads and smiled at the root in consideration. "With that," said Lara, "you don't even need the man." And they all laughed. The wind blew a hard gust, which pushed the rain under the structure and drowned out their laughter.

Kendal turned her attention from the five Garifuna women who'd allowed her into their circle and concentrated on the brown, thick root in her hand. Although the work of peeling and grating the cassava was long and tedious, it was a task she'd grown to love. And today, more than most days, with the rain pouring throughout the morning and now well into the afternoon, she'd needed to get out of her house, making the task especially welcome. As always, the steady movement of her hands slowed her mind and calmed the overload of sensation. She watched the flakes of brown as they flew around her—tiny brown moths winging their way to the sand—the calming scrape, scrape, scrape of her blade against the flesh. The tuber grew wet and sticky in her hand, and when it was white and glistening, she threw it in the vat of water and reached for another. She fought hard to resist the sticky wetness of the cassava juice—wanting to bring her fingers to her mouth and enjoy the bitter sensation—knowing that it was toxic until washed and processed. Would it kill her if she let go of caution?

"How's that baby?" Theresa asked Lara, who was sitting to Kendal's right and sweating in spite of the coolness in the air. Kendal looked up and smiled at the swell of Lara's belly and was glad hers was flat and empty. A baby—a tiny helpless soul—now, that was something she could fully consume, scrape away at until there was nothing left.

Lara wiped at her brow and rested her hand on her swollen stomach a moment. "Just fine. Loves kicking at her ol' mama."

"Her? You think it's a girl?"

"Damn well better be! I don't need another boy."

"Oh, it's a girl," said Dalia, who was bending over a large metal grater and grating the cassava into a fine cottage cheese. "You can tell by the way that baby is sitting."

The talk turned to children, and Kendal's attention returned to her cassava—the rhythm of women's voices a gentle, soothing melody in which the brown moths floated to the ground. There'd been a time when Kendal had played with dolls, pressed Barbie into Ken and dreamed of love and babies. Maybe it was the way Ken's arms would not bend or the fact that Barbie's expression never changed, but it seemed unreal and unconnected, the love that Barbie had for Ken.

She'd wanted, all her life, to have someone understand, to strip her relationships down to their very core, to feel an unwavering connection with another human—true and pure—to consume and be consumed, to scrape down to the very essence of a person, to open up her soul and lay it out for inspection. But this was not something that people tolerated. It was something unwelcomed and unattainable. People would not or could not display their very souls. And they certainly did not wish to look upon hers. And she had, with time, learned this; and she had, with time, accepted it. So no, there would be no babies to devour.

"Hey, ladies."

Kendal looked up from her cassava to see Mark standing at the back door of the restaurant.

"Good afternoon." His eyes fell on her, and his smile widened, and then his gaze went to Cordelia. "Not open today? Not cooking?"

"I'm sorry. Today, we're making the cassava flour. Tomorrow, the sun will be out, and we make the bread."

Mark stepped up to the circle of women and looked with curiosity at what they were doing. "That white cardboard stuff you make?" he asked with a smile. "This is what it's made from? Why am I not surprised?"

Cordelia's eyes narrowed at Mark. The women shook their heads in reprimand. The song of gentle clicks of tongues mingled with that of the rain. Kendal closed her eyes with a sigh.

Theresa's voice came out with firm good humor. "That white cardboard stuff! Well, it kept my ancestors alive when they were forced from their home, forced onto boats. Forced from Saint Vincent." She put her hands to her considerable chest and continued. "They put the cassava plant here, next to their skin, near their heart, where it was kept alive by their own sweat. And when those who survived the voyage reached the island of Roatan... Well, they had something to start with, something from their old life."

"Uh-oh." Mark grimaced sheepishly as he slowly stepped away and back into the restaurant. "Sorry. I think I'll just go now. Back, you know, out into the rain. Make myself a peanut butter sandwich. Yes, that's exactly what I'm going to do. Get really wet and eat peanut butter. Good afternoon, ladies."

And he was gone.

"Shit for brains," said Theresa, and they all laughed.

It was with relief that Mark approached King Kassava's and heard the distinctive voices of male activity. American football was on the TV. Loud and boisterous games of dominos were going on at several tables, with the tiles being slapped down with such enthusiasm that the tables rocked and the bottles of Belikin rattled dangerously. Off to one corner, three men beat on wooden drums, their dark braids swinging to the beat and adding a frenzied merriment to the place. Mark was further relieved when his eyes found Aaron and Melvin standing near a table as they watched one of the games of domino. He secured a beer and ordered chicken tortillas before heading over to the table.

Aaron and Melvin met his approach with smiles and nods. When Mark got close enough, he said, "I was just verbally attacked by a bunch of women. It was brutal."

"Yeah?" asked Melvin. "What did you do?"

"Me? Why is it I had to do something?"

Aaron and Melvin threw him a look.

"Okay, I insulted their cassava bread."

Melvin shook his head solemnly. "You are one dumb motherfucker. Almost anything but the cassava bread."

"Yeah, no kidding."

The men at the table exploded with shouts and moans. One of the men reached out and gathered up his winnings, shoving the bills into his pants pocket, while the others quickly gathered up the tiles, turned them over, and shuffled them noisily across the tabletop.

"Kendal was there," Mark told Aaron once the noise had settled down. "Up to her armpits in roots and peelings." Mark noted the flicker of some sort of pain, or maybe worry, that passed across Aaron's face, and he added, "She looked like she was doing okay."

Aaron nodded slightly, his gaze returning to the game. "Hey," he said after a few moments, tapping Mark's arm lightly with the butt of his beer bottle. "Do you want to use my phone now? Are you ready?"

Mark brought his beer to his lips and considered. "I don't know..." He took a long drink of his beer. Was he ready? What would he even say? *Hi, it's Mark. Remember me? How are you and fat fucking Bob?*

"Here," said Aaron, dropping his cell phone into Mark's front shirt pocket. "Take it. For the night. No one calls me anyway. Bring it back tomorrow."

"Zero zero one?"

"That's right."

Mark felt the weight of the phone in his pocket and was tempted to remove it. Maybe slip it into his back pocket, where it would be less conspicuous. Which is exactly what he did—away from his heart and next to his ass. He was laughing to himself at this thought when he saw Frank wave the plate of tortillas his way.

It was a couple hours later, with a few slow beers and food in his belly, that Mark made his way around the back of Kassava's to relieve the pressure of his full bladder. The daylight was beginning to fade, the rain slowing from a blowing downpour to a steady, straight descent. The village was beginning to come alive with a few brave souls walking the street with umbrellas; even braver souls pedaled bikes through the sludge. Preadolescent children skipped, wet and happy, through the mud puddles; wet and unhappy dogs slinked about for scraps of food; and not a chicken was anywhere in sight.

Mark stopped on his way back and looked up a ways at the lone figure standing in perfect stillness in the middle of the road. She was facing away, her umbrella closed and dangling from one of her hands, which hung limp from her sides. She was as wet as the slinking dogs. He considered going to her, took a few steps her way, but then he turned around and entered Kassava's.

Aaron was at a far table, involved in a hot, loud game of dominos, and Mark had to get close, bending down to Aaron's ear to tell him. Aaron looked up, his face twisting into concern, and he placed his hand on Mark's shoulder as he stood, handing him the tile he was about to place down and pushing him into his seat. "Here, play for me."

Mark watched Aaron leave, and then his eyes turned to the dotted lines of dominos with mild panic. The other men at the table grinned with pleasure and threw more money on the table. One of them punched Mark's arm lightly as he laughed over the noise. "It's your turn, fucking white boy."

Kendal turned to the sensation of warmth on her arm.

He was close, the rain dripping down his face. "What are you doing?" he asked gently.

"I love him."

He closed his eyes and smiled with understanding. "I know you do."

"I don't want to go home."

Now his face turned back to concern. Kendal could still feel the sticky cassava on her fingers—felt the coldness of the rain soaking into her sweater as it clung to her chest, could feel the drops slipping beneath the fabric, sliding down her back. And then she felt the heat of Aaron's hands as he pulled her to his chest, then the full heat of his arms, of his body, as they enveloped her. "I'm sorry," he said. And they lingered momentarily, for all the village to see, before he pulled one arm away and began to walk, his left arm still firmly around her shoulder so that her legs were forced to move along with his, toward home.

It was late evening now. The rain was slowing to a gentle patter on his roof. He sat on his bed and considered Aaron's phone. It lay, mixed up with his sheet, waiting with all the patience of an inanimate object, and Mark felt a loneliness sweep through the room. He picked it up, and it sparked into life as he flipped it open, lighting the dimness of the room. He flipped it closed and waited, watching the screen until it turned dark, before he flipped it back open to the burst of welcome light. He closed it again and waited. A tiny gecko chirped from somewhere above his head and was answered by another across the room.

"Are you talking about me?" Mark asked the darkness, and he was answered by silence. "Am I disturbing you?"

He stood up from the bed and paced gently, still clutching the phone in his hand. He walked to the window and peered into the darkness. He couldn't make out the ocean, but he could see the gentle swaying of the nearest palm. The gecko chirped above his head. He began to pace again.

"Damn it!"

He stopped, opened the phone, and pushed the keys without hesitation. He hit send and quickly brought the phone to his ear. He closed his eyes and held his breath as it began to ring.

Author Note: In this chapter, I'm not only exploring the relationship between women—how they are likely to come together in a task—but I'm also flirting with the relationship between an expat like Kendal and the local culture. In reality, it would be rare for an expat to be allowed into the fold—so to speak. As diverse as the population is in Belize, the various cultures are fairly segregated, much as it is all over the world. I like to think that Kendal is the exception!

Chapter 26: She Paused at Life and Held Her Breath Against the Waiting

Charlie opened his eyes and took her in. She was safe and warm and dry and sleeping peacefully beside him. He sighed as he recalled the dripping, cold state she was in last night. How she'd shivered for hours, even after a long, hot shower, and there'd been nothing he could do to make her warm. He was feeling, fully now, the weight of her despair, her loneliness, her conflicts. How she loved him and hated him. How she wanted him healthy and alive. How she longed for him to be dead and gone. Then there was his own despair of wanting the same things as she did. The despair of wanting Aaron gone and thankful that he wasn't, of wanting to tell her to be with him but not being able to and of hating her for making it an issue. If he could only take it back. If he'd only let it go, allowed it to remain just a scratch of irritation, a hint of suspicion. But now it was something big and unpleasant for everyone to see, and there was no place to go but where they were.

Before she even opened her eyes, she knew he was awake and looking at her. She felt the weight of his eyes as she felt the weight of the blanket on her skin, as she felt the solidness of the bed beneath her. She wanted to open her eyes and not see the old man that he'd become, not see the man that she'd betrayed and injured—but the man that she'd thrown her pack to, the man who'd run his hands over her body with wonder and amazement. The man who'd been her first and only love for so many years, who'd shown her how to love and how to trust and who'd calmed the chaos in her soul. And now she felt, as surely as she felt his eyes on her now, that it was all slipping away.

Then, suddenly, he was gone. She could feel the emptiness of the bed, and it was more real than what was truly real, so that her eyes popped open, and she was immediately rewarded by his face. "Oh, Charlie." She reached for him. "I thought you were gone."

"No," he said, easing into her embrace. "I'm here. I'm right here."

It was midmorning before the rain stopped; and then, quite suddenly, the sky was clear. As the sun burned away the puddles, Kendal made her way up the beach and located Mark wiping the wetness from his beach chair with his shirt. She briefly admired the bareness of his chest, which had gone from burned and blotchy to a fine, even brown; but then he looked up and saw her, and his smile focused her attention.

"Hey," he said softly. "How are you?"

"I'm good." The look on his face dissolved the awkwardness that she was feeling, and she smiled. "And you?"

He laid the now-wet shirt across the back of the chair and sent her a half smile. "Well, okay, I guess."

"What?" She drew closer and could tell he was bursting with some sort of news. "What did you do? Did you finally get laid?"

Mark laughed. "Hardly. No. I called home last night."

Kendal was taken aback. She studied his face for some sort of answer and finally said, "Well?"

"Well, what?" he teased her.

"What do you mean, 'well, what'?" she demanded. "What did she say? What did you say? Tell me. Tell me everything." When he still didn't answer, she drew closer and slapped his arm gently. "Tell me. You guys talked, didn't you? It went okay. I can tell."

"I don't know about okay," he said dismissively, "but it went."

"Just tell me, you jerk! All you ever want to do is talk about Cathy, and now that I'm begging you to, you clam up like a—like a big jerk!"

He sighed. "I just asked about the kids, told her where I was, and that was about it."

"*What?* Are you kidding me?"

He shrugged.

"I hate you!" she told him as she hit him again.

"Ow!" He rubbed at his arm. "Hey, I'm not here solely for your entertainment."

"Yes you are." She smiled. "As I am here for yours."

His face softened into a smile of admiration.

"It's true," she whispered as she stepped closer. She breathed into his ear, "We crack each other up." He laughed, and she felt joy rise to her throat—a sensation she needed and longed for. "I don't want you ever to go home," she said as she laughed. She stepped back and caught his eye, her joy slipping away. "Really."

He put his arms loosely around her shoulders. "Thank you." He kissed the top of her head.

With the closeness of that kiss came the sudden thought of his body easing into hers, followed by a deep sigh of sadness. She'd played him. A restless cat with a mouse, with no intention of ever going in for the kill. She'd enjoyed the knowledge that he wanted her, with little regard for how he might be affected. It had all been a game—a game, she truly believed, they'd both fully embraced. But had the rules ever been clear?

As he released her, she said, "You know, don't you, Mark, how sorry I am about the other night? At dinner... what Charlie said... I never meant for you to be dragged into all this. Maybe I could've been a better friend..."

He tilted his head at her. "Are you kidding me? I'd still be shit-faced, flat in the sand, if it weren't for you. And for Aaron. You've both been great, putting up with me"—he shook his head—"my whining. All this Cathy crap."

She smiled sadly. "So tell me. Tell me about Cathy. Give me something. Anything."

He shrugged. "She was alone. I think. She missed me. Sorta."

"She didn't say, 'Sorta.'"

"Well... actually, she didn't say she missed me, but her voice sounded, you know, lonely... or maybe just tired. I woke her up... with the time difference."

His face grew sad, and she put her hand on his arm.

"Hey, you know," he continued. "She didn't hang up. Hasn't sold my kids. She knows I'm alive. Progress was made."

"Aw, Mark.... She should be begging you to come home, begging for forgiveness." Then Kendal regretted her words because she could see the pain they caused, knew that that was what he'd wanted, hoped for, and not received. "I'm sorry."

"You know what?" He smiled. "Fuck her."

"That's right." Kendal stomped the sand with her foot. "Fuck her! I've always hated that stupid bitch! Fuck her!"

And then they were both overcome with giddy laughter until they were forced to sit on the beach chairs, wipe at their eyes, and catch their breath.

Author Note: This scene between Kendal and Mark is what I like to call a "breather." Literary-wise, the term is referred to as comic relief. Take three deep breaths, and keep reading!

Chapter 27: The Dogs Began to Bark, and the Babies Cried

Kendal kissed his cheek, which made her bag fall from her shoulder as she bent down, hitting her in the leg and flopping to the floor. She knelt down to retrieve it and stayed there, resting her hands on Charlie's knees and searching his face with her eyes. He smiled back from his place in his chair. She'd given him his lunch, tucked a blanket around his legs, as the weather was still cool, left a glass of water and his pills on the table—everything she had been doing on Fridays for the last six months—but she felt unsure, uncertain. "Are you sure you're okay with me taking off?"

"Kendal"—he smiled—"you know I've always needed Friday afternoons to myself. I've got all sorts of things I need to get done without some woman hanging around."

She laughed, because that was the way it had always been: the time he spent on the computer, catching up with correspondence, doing his paperwork, or fishing or playing cards with his friends. He used to go to town when all his work or play was done. They'd meet for dinner, after she'd spent the afternoon hiking or diving or shopping around town. She'd always get to King Kassava's first, read her novel, drink her Belikin; and she'd look up and he'd be there, telling his fish stories, complaining about his daughters or the sad state of his recent investments. And she would share her afternoon with him—remind him of the beauty of Antelope Falls, describe the marvelous sea turtle she'd seen, or show him the wonderful pineapple she purchased right from the back of the farmer's truck as it drove through the village. Then, when the sun had set and the coolness of the night had settled in, they'd walk arm in arm through the village, back home, where they would, more often than not, make love in their beautiful house by the sea.

"So you're good?"

He nodded. "Absolutely."

"So I'll bring you dinner. Fish or chicken? Rice and beans, or beans and rice?"

He laughed. "Stew beans and vegetable rice. Whatever fish is available."

Kendal stood up and rested her hand against his face. "Okay. Love you."

"Love you too."

And she left.

Kendal checked the hammocks hanging from the pier where Aaron could sometimes be found, swinging in the sea breeze and reading his books. When the hammocks proved empty, she made her way across the sand, past the swimming pool of Hamanasi, and along the row of buildings to the dive shop. She stepped quietly through the door and made her way through the neatly hung wet suits and BCDs and around to the office. The door was open, and he was sitting near the table doing paperwork. His hair, which was still damp from his morning dive, was pulled back from his face so that she could see the full beauty of his profile. She approached, undetected, and brought her lips down to his neck, where she smelled and then tasted the sea. He didn't jump at her touch, as if he somehow knew that she would be there. He swung around and captured her, pulling her into his lap. Their kiss was long and salty. "Play with me today," she whispered when her lips were free.

He shrugged with a smile. "What do you want to play?"

They both heard the voices of people growing closer, and she left his lap reluctantly. "I have a class in about a half hour," he was saying. "First-timers in the pool. You want to hang around until I'm done? Go for a short hike? Swim? Get dinner?"

She turned to see Melvin and one of the other divemasters bringing a small group of guests into the shop. Melvin's eyes met hers with a smile. Kendal felt Aaron's salty moisture on her lips and the pressure of all their eyes—which were on her. The painted red lips of the tall, pretty English woman who'd been talking to Melvin turned up slightly as she took Kendal in. The woman's eyes flitted across Kendal's long, sand-covered legs, past Charlie's oversized shirt, and lingered on her hair. Kendal's hand went automatically to the mass of twisted locks, feeling their roughness and finding a large strand of seaweed, which she collected and crushed between her fingers. Her eyes shifted away from the small crowd and back to Aaron, who was smiling up at the woman and surely taking in the woman's perfect auburn mane, imagining his fingers coursing through the softness.

Then Melvin was pulling BCD jackets from the hooks and handing them out for the guests to try on—helping the pretty woman with hers as if she were helpless. Masks and flippers were being pulled from their hooks, and everyone was talking—English, Garifuna, and American words streaming through the air—the walls of the dive shop too close, the sea air too far away, the pain as Kendal's chest tightened, the inability to breathe... There was the touch of Aaron's fingers against her hand, and he was saying something that was not possible to retrieve and separate from all the other words. And then her bare feet were moving with as much dignity as bare feet can when attached to sandy legs, and she was outside and sucking in the cool, fresh air as it blew in from the sea.

She walked back up the beach, against the surf, the pain easing in her chest, her breath returning to a slow and steady intake. She walked past Jungle Jeanie's, past her favorite clump of sea grapes, past her home, past Yugadah, past the small businesses and homes of the village that sat upon the shore, past the north end of the village, and then along the clean-swept beaches of the new development of Hopkins Bay Resort. And then even further past the lagoon, along the yet-to-be-developed stretch of sand, until the beach curved out toward the sea, until she was forced to wade through the water; and before the land disappeared into the sea, she sat near a sandy knoll dotted with a few scrub pines and sea grapes, her bright-colored bag hanging from an out-stretched branch above her head, the warm water lapping at her back, around her feet, between her upturned thighs, and then, and only then, did she allow herself to cry.

Charlie sent off a few emails, signed and faxed a couple documents. He saved and then closed out the Word document he'd been working on and stood up with some effort from the computer desk. He made his way to the kitchen counter and unplugged his cell phone from the charger. Sitting on the kitchen stool with a soft moan, he scrolled through his contacts until he reached Claire and hit the send button. The phone rang four times before it went to voicemail.

"Hi, Claire, it's your dad. Just calling to say hi. Are you still planning to try to come for a visit? Maybe after Christmas? Well... call me back sometime. Tell Mike hi, and give those kids a kiss from me." He disconnected the call and found Julie's name in his contacts. She answered on the second ring.

"Dad! How are you?"

Charlie smiled at the sound of her voice, crisp and no-nonsense but mingled with true affection. "Good. I'm good. How's that grandson of mine?"

"Oh, he's great. He loves that drum you sent him. Thank you very much." And she laughed. "The least you could have done was include a bottle of Advil."

Charlie laughed. "That was made right here in the village by a friend of mine."

"Really? It's great. Jack plays it every day. But for Christmas, maybe something small and quiet."

Charlie could hear her suck in a breath, undoubtedly from the end of a cigarette.

"Dad, how are you? How are you feeling?"

"I thought you told me that you quit." He heard her exhale.

"I did, for a while. Are you going to answer me or not?"

"I believe that question was already answered." She sighed, and Charlie began to regret that he'd made the call.

"It's not wrong for me to worry about you, Dad. Have you given any more thought to what we talked about? Coming home to Miami? You can stay with us."

Charlie closed his eyes, and it was his turn to sigh.

"You know, if you're here, you can get on the national transplant list. You're not that old."

"Dammit, Julie! Why is it almost every time I call, you bring up something that you know damn well isn't going to happen?" He'd tempered his voice, tempered his frustration, but still, he heard her sharp intake of breath.

"I'm sorry, Dad..."

He could hear the pain in her voice, knew that she was on the verge of tears, puffing on her cigarette with all she had and tapping her lacquered nails against her desk. "Why don't you come see me? After Christmas," he said gently. "Let me get a look at that grandson of mine."

"Sure. We could do that." There was a pause. "And Kendal? How's Kendal?"

Charlie smiled. "She's good. Very good. Thank you for asking."

"Well, tell her I said hello, will you? I'll look into flights and let you know."

"Okay. Good. I'll let you get back to work." It was after he'd hung up the phone, after he'd plugged it back into the charger, that he realized he hadn't really said goodbye.

Kendal sat at her usual table at King Kassava's, drips of water rolling down her Belikin, leaving a puddle on the table. She held the scant final pages of her novel in her right hand, ignoring her beer and biting her lower lip as she took in the final words of the story. She flipped to the last page, reading the words and then closing the book as she pressed it to her chest. Her eyes went up, and he was there, smiling at her, his blond hair washed and dry and flowing freely around his face.

"Was it good?" he asked.

She nodded her head.

"I looked for you. After I was done. Couldn't find you anywhere. Did you find someone else to play with? Maybe Mark? I never found him either. I'm sorry I had that stupid pool dive. How are you? Are you okay?"

Kendal pulled her feet from the other chair, pushing it out slightly toward Aaron.

"Sorry." He sat. She pushed her beer his way, and he reached for it, trapping her fingers in the exchange. "Are you okay?"

She nodded. She didn't trust her voice—didn't trust her mind to put the words in an order that made sense. The words of the novel were still swirling around with her own words, their story twisted about with hers.

"Is it too late to do something now? We could at least get dinner. Will you eat with me? I know Charlie's expecting you with his dinner, but we could eat now. Eat early? Frank's got some snapper and conch."

She brought her other hand into the mix of their fingers, the beer still somewhere in between the two of them. She didn't care that the others in the restaurant were surely watching, seeing their hands mingling with the beer, seeing her eyes not leaving his. They all knew. Everyone knew, and nobody cared. They were nothing more than mild Saturday-morning gossip at the bus stop, and even that news was probably old and stale.

"Conch. I think Charlie would like the conch." The words came out, and they seemed to be in the correct order. "Me? I'll have the snapper. With you. I'll eat snapper with you."

He was on the beach, in one of their wooden beach chairs, and he was enjoying the last sun of the day, the shadows stretching across the sand as the sun set behind the house. Out in the sea, he could see the gentle breach of the water as a manatee foraged for dinner. A pair of pelicans flew close to one another, their bellies almost bumping into the sea as they made their way north. He took a deep breath and felt the discomfort, felt the burn in his chest, and he regretted that pineapple. Pineapples—they never failed to cause him heartburn. What he'd really wanted was a mango—a beautiful, wonderful fruit that dropped from the trees like raindrops in the spring. But it was not spring; it was early winter, and the mangoes were just tiny green promises that he was unlikely to ever see fulfilled.

Charlie considered leaving the beach, making his way back upstairs to his bottle of TUMS, when numbness in the fingers of his left hand joined the pain in his chest, a sensation not likely caused by the innocent pineapple, and he looked around the beach and saw not a soul. Then, as the nausea hit, he thought of his computer, of all that he'd been working on. Almost everything was done and signed and notarized, in neat little piles—how odd his thoughts would turn to lawyerly things. But it wasn't all quite done, and he thought about Kendal chopping him up and tossing the pieces to the hungry, waiting crocs, which actually made him laugh, because only Kendal would come up with such a thing.

He was on his feet now and heading toward the surf, the pain now snaking down his left arm. It wasn't that he had a problem with crocs, or even suits for that matter, but he had a problem with her finding him, with the drama of his death on his face and the fire truly gone from his eyes, so if he had the choice, which he did, he would not choose crocs or suits.

The kayak was heavier than he recalled, and the sand was unyielding as he pulled it, with only his right arm, toward the waiting sea. He had to stop and rest—sit his body down on the bow and gasp for air. It wasn't long before the pain softened, and he was about to rise when he heard his name.

"Do you need help, Charlie?" It was Mark's face he looked up to in the fading light.

"Yes." He managed to sound normal. "I'm going for a little kayak. Could you help me with the boat?"

"It's almost dark. Are you sure you want to go?"

"Evening is best." He was on his feet and leaning slightly toward the pain.

"Are you okay? You don't look so well."

Charlie brought his hand to Mark's arm and grasped it lightly. "Will you help me, please? With the boat?" He watched as Mark considered his request, took in the urgency of his words, and Charlie could see the doubt on his face. "Please?"

Charlie saw Mark make up his mind and reach for the boat. He pulled the bow until the kayak was bouncing gently in the surf. He helped Charlie into the seat and handed him the paddle. "Do you want me to wait until you're done? To help you out?"

Charlie smiled up from the kayak. "No. Kendal will be here. Thank you, Mark." He started to paddle away but then turned back toward the shore. "Oh, Mark!"

"Yes?" Mark asked, the water lapping softly at his calves, the sun setting behind his back.

"Go home. You don't belong here. Go home. Try to make it work with your wife, and even if it doesn't, be there for your kids. Go home to your kids."

And the irony, that those would be his last words, did not escape him.

The sun was setting to her right as she walked, the sky pink and streaky, its splendor stretching to her left—to the east—to the sea. Her bag of takeout for Charlie was banging gently against her leg, and her multi-colored knapsack rested lazily on her shoulder. And it was those characters, the ones from her novel, that were flitting about in her head when she looked out to the darkening sea and saw the small craft, out far from shore, almost indistinguishable from the water. It was a beautiful thing, this lone boat in the fading light, a lone figure on board. What a lovely view of the world this person must be taking in, as surely, he was gazing across the water toward shore—toward the setting sun, toward Belize, with the Maya Mountains pressed against the sky. She knew that there was no prettier thing to behold, and she wished she could join this being and watch until the last glow from the sun disappeared into the mountains, until the darkness won out and the moon rose into the sky. Then she watched with wonder as this figure seemed to rise up and out of the boat, disappearing into the sea. But it must be a visual trick, as it was nearly dark and too far out and too late for a swim.

It was not until she reached her beach, walked into her home, and was unable to locate her husband that she returned to the beach, saw the tracks in the sand, noted the missing kayak, and fell to her knees. Then the dogs began to bark, and the babies cried, the chickens flew from their roosts, the men looked up from their beers, and the women paused over brightly colored rows of vegetables at the sound of her agony.

Author Note: What do you think? Would Charlie have chosen a different path if things had been different? Would he have waited for help? Did he do what he did more for himself or for Kendal?

Chapter 28: Somewhere, Nowhere, and Everywhere

Mark watched as the men attached the motor to the boat and dragged it to the surf. It was Noel's boat, and Frank was there. Mark didn't know the others, but it was four men that piled into the boat. Aaron stood close and conflicted—standing between the boat and the cluster of women that surrounded her sorrow. The boat fired into life and moved away through the soft waves. Mark watched the bouncing lights as the flashlights the men held grew smaller. They could hear her sorrow, over the sound of the boat, over the sound of the soothing voices of women—a sound not that different than what had brought them there.

"I helped him," Mark said, his eyes flicking to Aaron and then back to the sea. "I gave him my arm. I helped him into the boat." Aaron didn't seem to be listening. "He didn't look well. I knew better. I even handed him the paddle."

Aaron took a step closer to the cluster of women. Mark looked away from the sea and saw a dog dragging the plastic bag through the sand—away from the cluster—and watched as it tore into the container and greedily consumed the contents.

"Jesus," he said, reaching for Aaron, putting his hand on the other man's shoulder as much in comfort as in keeping himself upright.

Then suddenly, the cluster was chattering and moving—as a single unit, it chattered and moved across the sand, up the stairs, and into the house.

They sat in the sand, between the sea and the house. Aaron sat close, so close that Mark could feel the heat of his body. Everyone else had gone home to get some sleep before the first light of dawn, when they would try again. They were waiting, waiting for the first light of dawn. Other than the soft sound of women moving around, the house behind them had grown quiet. Someone had brought them coffee, which sat cold and untouched in the sand in front of them. Mark glanced at Aaron. His head was down on his arms, which were draped and crossed on his upturned knees. He may have been asleep. Mark hoped he was. Mark could sense the ghost crabs creeping across the sand in the dark, could swear he felt the sand shift around his feet as they drew near. He tried not to let it freak him out. They were only crabs, and crabs were so much less freaky than death.

Other boats had gone out, hours ago—boats from Hamanasi, other boats from the village. Aaron had finally been able to move and go out on one of the boats. Mark had gone along, sweeping his flashlight beam across the eerie waters, sucking in his breath, an uncomfortable shot of adrenaline pulsing through his body each time the tiniest of objects filled his circle of light. They'd found nothing but the kayak, which now sat empty on the beach in front of them. Mark closed his eyes to the faint image of the kayak but reopened them quickly because every time his eyes fluttered shut, the image of Charlie flowing with the sea swept through his mind.

Aaron hadn't said more than a dozen words to him all night, as if he were in shock or angry. Was he angry? Did he blame Mark? What sort of person helps an old, sick man into a kayak and sets him out into a darkening sea? He might as well have pushed him out of the boat himself.

"I loved him." Aaron's words came out so soft that Mark almost didn't pick them up. "I love them both. And it's my fault."

He awoke to the sun well up in the sky and Aaron gone. Mark was slumped into the sand and on his side. He could see his bare feet resting near the overturned coffee mugs, the sand dark and wet between his toes; a tiny circle of Aaron's cigarette butts stood in the sand next to the mugs. He sat up and could see the boats moving slowly through the waters, out far in front of the house. He looked back and up to the house. Cordelia's dark, shiny face was there, leaning over the railing, peering out to sea.

"How is she?" he called softly.

Cordelia's gaze shifted to him, and she shook her head sadly. "Come on up here and get yourself some coffee."

Mark picked up the two coffee mugs and made his way to the side of the house, up the stairs, and onto the veranda. He'd never been in Charlie and Kendal's house, and it felt odd and wrong. He lingered on the veranda, peering into the house through the open French doors, handing Cordelia the dirty mugs in exchange for a hot new cup.

"Come on in," she told him.

He looked into the living room and on into the kitchen, which was open, defined only by cabinetry and located in the back of the house. Two women he didn't know, one Garifuna and the other white, sat at the small eating table in front of the kitchen island, talking softly. The house was simple and nice, with two chairs facing the sea, one of old and beaten leather, the other a delicate paisley print. There was a small couch against the left-hand wall, facing a small TV, which sat alone and almost out of place on its little stand. A few rustic paintings, from local artists no doubt, hung from the walls, a braided rug thrown here and there, minimal knickknacks, minimal female flair. He looked at the closed door off the back left side of the living room and then at the partially open door on the right. Cordelia looked to the right and said, "She's sleeping. Nurse Ruth gave her something. You can come on in."

"Thanks, but I think I'll just go back. You know, back to the beach."

There was nothing to do but to sit on the beach and watch as the hours rolled by. Aaron came and went. Soft white clouds appeared high in the perfect blue sky, which slowly shifted to a fine, thin cloud covering. A threatening dark cloud bank crept in and hugged but never strayed from the northeast edge of the sea. Various foods appeared. Someone brought beer, and Mark helped himself. A makeshift card table was set up on the beach, and some of the men played quiet games of dominos. The sun dipped toward the Maya Mountains. The boats had given up long ago and returned with only living souls. Someone started a fire. Children rolled in the sand and splashed in the sea. Someone sang in a deep, soft voice. Dogs sniffed around for scraps. Someone beat gently on a drum. Women came and went from the house. Then, one by one, as the dusk turned into night, they all drifted away and back to their lives. All except for a couple women holding sentry in the house; and Aaron and Mark, who sat close in the sand, between the sea and the house. Mark peered out at a seemingly empty sea. Aaron dipped his head and cried, almost silently, into the sand.

Author Note: Regardless of cultural differences, financial disparity, and ideals, a village is a village, and its people come together to help one another when there's a death. They support and grieve—even if they barely knew the person. So many experiences—whether they be of pleasure or pain—are collective in a small community. And maybe even in a large one—like the collective pain of a pandemic.

Chapter 29: Rights and Responsibilities

"I remember I was sitting right here, maybe in this very chair, when the son of a bitch—he was even kinda old back then—came strolling in, grinning from ear to ear like a lovesick teenager." Frank laughed and brought the Belikin to his lips.

"I remember that," said Noel, smiling, his dark eyes drifting away with the memory. "We all knew. We'd seen him walking around town with her. We all knew the bastard had gone and got himself laid. She was something, even then, even though she was all skinny and almost bald, with a sorta crazy look in her eye. But I'll tell you what." He sat back and pointed his cigarette in the general direction of the men. "There wasn't a man in town, including me, that wouldn't have traded places with Charlie in a heartbeat."

The five men sat way in the back of the bar, around two small tables they'd pushed together. The restaurant had closed several hours ago, and all the locals and tourists had given up on their drinking and gone home or back to their hotels. It was Sunday night, and Charlie had been gone two days. Mark looked from Noel to Aaron, who was sitting across from him. Aaron was smiling gently, clutching his beer with two hands as he leaned on the table; he didn't seem terribly concerned that the talk had turned to Kendal.

"You know," said Clement, the fifth man at the table, who was a tall and ropey expat from Canada. He'd lived here for years, struggling to support himself and his substantial intake of alcohol by taking tourists out fishing. He pulled absently at his long white mustache as he talked.

"He gave me the money I needed to fix my fishing boat. I tried to talk to him once about paying some of it back. He nearly bit my head off."

"He could be a real son of a bitch at times," said Noel. "Remember the time he got so mad at that real estate salesman? We almost had to haul him off to jail." The men laughed.

"Yeah," said Frank. "He had a hell of a temper, especially when he was younger. But when he met her—well, it changed him somehow. Now, my woman..." He laughed. "She's just made me more of a bastard."

"If that ain't the fucking truth!" exclaimed Noel. He raised his beer and emptied the bottle in one long swallow. When he was done, his face grew grave. "Do you think it was an accident? A man with years of experience?" His eyes turned to each of his companions, and his question was answered with sad shakes of their heads. All except for Aaron, who was giving his full concentration to the label of his beer.

"Has anyone seen her?" Clement asked, and all eyes turned to Aaron.

When Aaron didn't say anything—his eyes never straying from the bottle in his hands—Noel said, "My wife says she's bad. Can't get out of bed on her own... not eating."

"I heard her parents are coming."

"Yeah, I heard that too."

"What about Charlie? Is anyone going to do something for him? A funeral? Some sort of service?" asked Clement.

"Well, that would be up to Kendal, I'd say. She's not up to anything," Noel said as he twirled his empty beer bottle noisily around on the table.

Aaron reached out and gently brought it to a rest. Noel looked at Aaron, furrowing his brow and narrowing his eyes while Frank spoke.

"He's got family in the States. Daughters. Remember? They've come here a few times. Grandkids. He showed me a photo once."

Aaron pushed his chair away from the table and stood. The men watched as he turned from the group and left without a word. Mark's eyes traveled around the table, and then he smiled faintly at the men and went after Aaron.

"I have a right to be there!" Aaron spat the words at him as soon as he'd caught up. Aaron was walking quickly down the road with a determination and a purpose he'd not shown in the last two days. But then he said softly, "Don't you think?"

"I'm sure she wants you there," Mark offered weakly. "Needs you there," he added.

They walked in silence, closing the distance between Kassava's and Kendal's. Mark contemplated what else to say, feeling the need to say something else to try to ease away Aaron's anger—his uncertainty. "I think Charlie would want you there," he finally uttered.

Aaron stopped and turned to him. Even in the darkness, Mark could see his error. "You barely knew the man! How the fuck would you know what he'd want?"

Mark felt his own anger, stood up a little straighter, and faced Aaron. "I knew him well enough to know he loved her. That he wouldn't want her not to be able to get out of bed. Not to be able to eat. And if what she needs—what might help her—is you, well, so be it."

Aaron sighed, turned from him in the dark. "That's a lot. It's a lot. You know... to be that for someone..." But he began to walk, slowly, with less determination, toward Kendal.

Mark stood in the middle of the road and watched him walk away. After a few yards, Aaron stopped, turned to him, and said, "You're coming, aren't you?"

She rocked with gentleness. She closed her eyes and couldn't hear the sad noise that escaped from her lips but only felt the gentle swaying of the sea and the full loss of him. And when she opened her eyes, reality didn't alter—he was gone as truly as she was not. But then, to not be sure... to expect to open her eyes and see him there. Better to feel his death—its smell, its wetness, its weight, its coolness—with every part of her body. To feel the solidness of him—to cut his death into little pieces and throw it to the crocs—to taste it on her fingers, to see it, to run it through her hair, spread it across her face, to know without a doubt that he was truly gone. All she had were the hundreds of brightly colored fish of her imagination, nipping at his death; the tiny crabs taking away their share—his death being spread across the sea in so many little pieces—his life, in so many little pieces, spread across the sea.

She rose from her place on the floor, in the corner, to go to him—to walk into the sea and feel his death—his life—flowing around her. She made it as far as the living room before she was stopped and confronted.

"What can I get you? Would you like some tea? Lara brought a nice soup. Will you eat some?"

The questions slapped at her senses, confusing her purpose, causing her to withdraw back to the safety of her corner—to the safety of her movement—to the gentle swaying of sadness.

They entered the house with a soft tap on the frame of the open French doors. Mark could tell by the ease with which Aaron moved through the space that he'd been here many times. Theresa, Aaron's landlady, the woman who'd set Mark straight regarding cassava bread, looked up from her work. Her lips smiled with welcome.

"Hi, Theresa," said Aaron quietly.

"Aaron."

He sat near her on the couch, his eyes resting on the fabric in her hands.

Mark stood by the door and watched the small cloud of bugs that swarmed around the floor lamp.

"I have some nice soup from Lara. Would you men like some?"

"I have a right to be here," Aaron said.

She put her sewing down and gazed at him. "Yes, just as we all do," she answered. "A right. A responsibility."

"Is it true—she's not good?"

"It's true."

Then there was a silence, which was soon filled with the soft sound of pain. Aaron looked toward the open bedroom door. "Let me stay with her tonight." He looked up at Mark. "We both will."

Mark walked into the room, crossed over toward the kitchen, and sat at the eating table.

Theresa looked from one man to the next. "She needs her medication in an hour," she said, indicating the bottles that sat on the table.

Mark lifted the bottles and read the labels. He looked up at Aaron, back to Theresa. He hadn't known, would have never guessed. He could tell from the meds—from the dates—that these were drugs she'd been on for some time.

"Nurse Ruth says she needs more. More than what it says on the bottle. It's written down on the table."

"Go on home, Theresa," Aaron said. "Go home to your family. We've got this for the night."

Theresa folded up her sewing and stood. "Lara will be here in the morning, at seven." But then she looked at him with uncertainty.

Aaron stood. "We're good. We got this. We'll be here when Lara gets here."

"Did you know?" asked Mark after Theresa had left. He was toying with the medication bottles, slowly tossing one of the bottles from one hand to the next. "About her illness?"

Aaron was still standing near the door where he'd bidden Theresa goodnight. "Yes. I've always known," he said absently, his eyes not on Mark but on the entrance to the bedroom.

"How did you know?"

Aaron's eyes turned to him. "I don't know. It wasn't a secret. Not something really talked about, but something everybody knew."

Mark felt stupid. With all his training, all his education, he was still just plain stupid—assuming that crazy people were crazy people, that you could spot them in a crowd, that they weren't just people but something different, something obvious. And here was Kendal, more real than anyone he'd ever met, someone who'd befriended him in the worst moment of his life—listened and laughed, had made him laugh—someone he loved in his own perverse way; and she loved him too, as a person, as a fellow human being, as a fellow living thing.

He watched as Aaron crossed the room and disappeared into the bedroom, leaving the door open. Mark sat at the table for a long time, staring at the medication bottles and thinking about the hundreds of similar drugs he'd given out. Of all the people he didn't know who were suffering or all the people he did know but didn't know were suffering—and then of his own miserable suffering, which everybody knew about—if they stood there long enough. Then he was done with thinking, and he got up and moved onto the couch, where he lay his body down, closed his eyes of his own free will for the first time in two days, and let sleep take him over.

She rocked with gentleness. With her eyes closed, she couldn't hear the soft noise of sadness that escaped from her lips. Then she felt his presence, the heat from his body, his smell, the strength of his arm around her shoulder—kept her eyes closed to the reality of him. She leaned slightly into his heat and then into his solid stillness.

Author Note: In the end, the dogs wander off, the children need tending, work needs to be done, and the mourners are left to mourn while their sup-

porting community struggles with what more they can do... until they finally shrug and move on fully.

Chapter 30: A Rose by Any Other Name

Mark watched as they came into the village like a small thunder, disrupting the flow and the rhythm of the place. It was a soft and efficient rhythm which they disrupted—the rhythm of people coming and going, never leaving her alone, expecting nothing and everything. And she was getting better—eating small sips of soup when it was brought to her lips, small words coming from her mouth when she was asked something—no more rocking in the corner.

First, it was the daughters on Monday—driving into the village in their rented vehicle, stepping out of the car as if stepping into controversy. A quick trip to the house to apparently inventory the damage and then back to the center of town to corner Noel at Kassava's. Mark peered over his beer and watched as Noel sat on a stool and smiled with sympathy and nodded and patted the swell of his stomach.

"What are you doing to find my father?" the taller and older of the women demanded.

Noel smiled and moved his hand along his stomach. "Well, ma'am, we searched the sea. For days, we searched."

"And why did you stop?" Her shoes tapped against the sandy floor of the bar—the pain, the stress flowing from her face as she spoke. Her sister, standing near, was biting at her long, painted nails and trying not to cry.

Noel looked over to Mark with some sort of plea, as if he, also being an American, could make them understand.

"Charlie was a friend. We tried. I'm sorry..." Noel said sadly, lifting his hands toward the heavens. "There are some things that aren't meant to be found."

And then the younger sister did cry, in deep, gut-wrenching sobs, and Noel rubbed his belly, and Mark looked away and out into the street, but he heard, just as clear as day, Noel's words over the sobs.

"The sea, it's a good place. The place that I would want to be."

Then there was the bigger disruption on Tuesday—the larger wave of her parents. Her father—tall, well-built for an older man, confident in his movements—walked into the village as someone who could easily change the place, take it over and make it something better. Her mother was smaller, less substantial, but still tall for a woman—with an air of someone who not only stands behind her husband but helps to push him along. And, unlike the daughters, these two dressed as if they knew where they were—no high heels or white pressed pants—making their force somehow more to contend with. They didn't waste their energy on Charlie and where he might be now but only on their daughter, going right to the house, surprising Judith, who was cleaning fish on the veranda and talking to her older boy about his future. They looked up from the guts of the fish, from the words mothers give to their children, and took in this force making its way onto the veranda.

It was Judith's older boy who told Frank, who told Aaron, who had just come in from a dive and was grabbing a quick bite of food with Mark. So that it was the two of them that walked down the beach to Kendal's, Mark in an old pair of cutoffs and his favorite Ohio State T-shirt; and Aaron, who hadn't bothered to button his shirt after the dive, still salty and damp from the sea, the creases from his dive mask still etched into his face. They stepped onto the veranda and into the house. They saw Judith with the parents, trying to talk to them in her heavy Garifuna accent, standing back toward the kitchen, looking small and dark and swallowed up. Judith turned at the two men's approach, looked at them with profound relief, and eagerly returned to her dead fish.

"Hi, I'm Aaron," he said, stepping fully into the house and through the living room, taking the man's hand into his. He tilted his head back and said, "This is Mark."

"Richard Sibley," Kendal's father said, taking Aaron's hand and then reaching for Mark's. Mark shook the man's hand. "My wife, Anne," said Richard.

Mark smiled at Kendal's mother, who put out her hand, so he shook that one too. He could see the resemblance. It was Kendal's eyes that looked back at him; it was Kendal's smile that quickly sprouted on this woman's face and then disappeared into something close to worry. Then they all put their hands to their sides.

Richard waited. Waited for some sort of explanation of why they were there. Mark looked at Aaron, who seemed to be waiting for a similar explanation from them.

"You're friends of Charlie's?" Anne Sibley finally ventured.

"Well, yes. Of both of them. Kendal and Charlie..." Aaron looked to the bedroom door as his voice trailed away.

Mark followed his gaze, and he could just see the top of Kendal's head, her crazy dreadlocks spread across the sheets. Was she sleeping? He looked away and back to the small group. They were all looking toward the bedroom.

Anne Sibley was suddenly moving. She moved away from the kitchen and into the living room area—away from the view of the bedroom. "Come. Please. Sit," she said formally, indicating the couch and chairs. "Can I get you something? Coffee? Tea?"

It was then that Aaron must have noticed the open door—off the other side of the living room. He moved to it, and as he shut it, Mark saw that it was Kendal's studio. Aaron turned from the door and met the looks of her parents.

"She never keeps it open. It's always closed. She doesn't like anyone in there," he said. "Even Charlie had to ask, you know"—he gave an easy laugh—"before he could go in." Aaron moved away from the closed door and sat on the couch, leaning forward, resting his arms on his knees. "No, thank you, about the coffee. We're fine. Right, Mark? Or maybe you want something?"

Mark shook his head, but what he really wanted was beer. He hadn't quite had a chance to finish the one he was having with his lunch.

"Do you want a beer?" Aaron added. "I'm sure there's some in the fridge. Charlie always has beer in the fridge."

Mark smiled gratefully at his friend but shook his head. He sat next to Aaron on the couch. Richard sat in the old leather chair and Anne in the other.

"You sure I can't get you something?" asked Anne, running her fingers nervously through her short-cropped hair.

"It's a shame about Charlie," Richard said, allowing them to ignore his wife's question.

Aaron nodded his head. "So, I guess there's a lot of stuff to do. You know—legal stuff. He has papers, you know, by the computer. He told me he had everything written down. His daughters are here. Have you seen them yet? They're staying at Jaguar Reef. Do you know where that is? Where are you staying? I could get you a room, you know, at Hamanasi. Get you a good discount. How long are you staying?" He stopped, took a breath, and waited for an answer.

Anne and Richard looked at one another. "Well," Anne said, choosing to answer the final question. "We're staying until we can get Elizabeth's things together. A couple of days...?"

"Elizabeth?"

"Our daughter," said Richard.

"Kendal?"

"Her name is Elizabeth. I don't know where the hell Kendal came from."

"The name or the woman?"

"What?"

"The name or the woman?" Aaron repeated.

Richard gave Aaron a hard look. "The name. My daughter—the woman in the other room—her name is Elizabeth. It's always been Elizabeth." And his voice grew soft and sad.

Aaron sighed and put his head down in his hands. "You know, she's getting better. Every day." He looked up from his hands. "We're taking care of her. All of us. She's getting better. Every day."

"She's not eating. Hasn't bathed. Not speaking..." Anne said.

"No. She is. She ate some last night. She talks. When she has something to say. She—"

"She needs to be somewhere where she can get help, somewhere safe," Richard said.

Aaron stood up. "She's safe. We're taking care of her. She's never alone. We're—"

Richard stood up also. "Who's taking care of her?" His words were angry, belittling. "A bunch of strangers in the middle of nowhere?"

"We're not strangers. The village. The village is taking care of her."

Richard pointed his finger at Aaron. "Don't be giving me a bunch of Hillary it-takes-a-village bullshit. We're taking her home, where she can be properly cared for."

"Cared for? Where? In some fucking nuthouse? Truly by strangers!"

Richard brought his hands to his sides and glared at Aaron. Aaron didn't look away. "Who are you, exactly?" he demanded.

Aaron looked away. "I'm... I'm Aaron." He looked around the house. "This is her home. This is where she lives. You can't take her away." He looked back at Richard. His words came out as a low and dangerous hiss: "This is where she lives, you motherfucker, where *Kendal* lives."

"I'm going to kill that bastard! I swear to God, if you hadn't got me out of there, I would have killed the fucker right there!" They were walking rapidly down the beach toward Hamanasi. Mark had never seen Aaron this angry. "Do they think she's twelve years old? She's lived here for ten fucking years. She's never been sick. Never fallen apart. Now her husband dies and she's fucking sad, and they think she's fucking crazy and needs to be locked up in some fucking place! It's just an excuse. They want her back! They just fucking want her back, and now they think they can swoop in, just days after her fucking husband dies, and drag her back to the States, where she would truly die. She can barely stand to go to Dangriga! Did you know that? Fucking Dangriga stresses her out!"

Mark's heart was beating rapidly now, trying to keep up with Aaron. They'd passed Hamanasi, and he continued to rant until they ran out of beach. Aaron kicked at a mangrove and then brought his hands to its branches and shook the tree, causing its many branches to rattle, its roots to clatter. Some of its leaves fluttered down into the sea. Aaron let his head come down as he held on to the branches, breathing deeply now and silent.

Mark was afraid to speak, afraid of what Aaron might do if he said the wrong thing. And Mark seemed to be quite good at saying the wrong thing, so that several minutes went by before he grew brave enough to speak. "I think you need to go to Kendal," he said carefully. "Talk to her. Only Kendal can make them understand."

And Aaron did not whip around and strike him or scream in his face but continued to look down into the sea and nod his head in sad agreement.

Author Note: Until I wrote this chapter, I had no idea that Kendal's name really wasn't Kendal.

Chapter 31: A Glass Azure Sea

She woke. It was dark and seemed to be the middle of the night. Cordelia was there and smiled at her and brought a glass to her lips. "Drink."

So she drank.

The next time she woke, it was Aaron who brought the glass to her lips and gave her a pill, which she swallowed. It was dawn. The sun was just showing itself, the sea just visible in its pink-blue glow. She shook her head in confusion. Had her parents been there? Then he was lifting her from the bed, and she resisted.

"You need to get up now," he whispered into her ear. "It's time. You can be sad. You can be sad as long as you want, but you need to get up now." She was on her feet, unwillingly, and he was easing her into the bathroom. "They want to take you. From Belize. From me." He gently lifted her shirt from her waist and carefully freed it from her body. "You need to show me how strong you are." He pulled the sweats from her hips and set her on the toilet.

When she was done, he was there, lifting her in his nakedness. The water was running, and then the warmth was cascading over her head and down the curves of her chest, her back, sliding down her legs. His hands were there, slipping over her skin, the bar of soap sliding smoothly down her back, coming forward, his hand and the soap, over her shoulders and under her arms, around her breasts and easing across her stomach, between her thighs, then down her legs and carefully coming back up and gently cleansing her folds, the soap foaming in her pubic hair. Then the smell of her shampoo floated about her, and his hands were pressing into her scalp, the sensation of fingers cleaning away her distress, the taste of shampoo easing into her mouth, his arms around her now and her tears mixing with lather. Then his lips were brushing against hers, slipping over her eyes.

"I love you, Kendal. I have from that very first moment, and I know you can do this. You can get better. Don't let them make you go."

Then the water was off, and he was wrapping her up in the softness of a towel, rubbing gently at the wetness, his arms around her shoulders, easing her out of the bathroom. He lifted a robe from a hook and let the towel drop to the floor as he brought the robe to her shoulders.

"No," she cried. "It's Charlie's."

"It doesn't matter," he said as he brought her arms into its folds. "You can be closer to him." He wrapped the smell of her husband about her and led her to the living room. He settled her into Charlie's old leather chair. "I'm going to make you some eggs. Is scrambled okay? And then we're going to get you dressed. I'll make you coffee. Or would you rather have tea? And when they come, in a little bit, then you can tell them. You can tell them that this is your fucking home. I think tea would be better, you know? And then we're going to go to the beach. And when they come, you'll be on the beach and sipping tea and looking like this is where you belong, like this is your home..."

He continued to prattle away in the kitchen as he cooked, and Kendal sat in Charlie's chair that was now her chair, in her house that was now only her house, and peered with calmness at a glass azure sea.

Author Note: Here we are starting to see just what kind of man and what kind of lover Aaron is. I especially love what he does in the next chapter!

Chapter 32: A Good Man

Mark walked slowly along the shore. The darkness was settling in, the evening breeze picking up; soft waves were seeking out his bare feet, but he made no move to avoid the mild wet intrusion.

"That's right, honey, I'm walking along the sea right now. I can see a big fat pelican." He laughed. "No. I don't see a fish hanging out of its mouth. But he's fat, like he's eaten a lot of fish." He stopped and closed his eyes in pain and pressed the cell phone a little closer to his ear. "Soon. You know, soon. You see, I have this friend I've made..." A smile. "Yes, it's a *boy* friend. Anyway, well, you see, someone died, and I need to be here just a little longer... for my friend. But I promise you, I'll be home for Christmas." He laughed again. "Yeah, I like that song too." He began to walk. "Sure, go ahead and sing it, then let me talk to your sister..."

Aaron ordered rice and beans, and Mark ordered the stew chicken with beans and rice. Melvin had already eaten but was pleased to join them for a Belikin, especially if Mark was buying, which he'd said he was. They were eating at Yugadah. There was one other group of diners—American tourists, who had just come in and were taking the place in with wonderment. Cordelia went to their table with a small theatrical bow, flaring her skirts with her hands and smiling her best smile.

"Welcome to Yugadah. Welcome to Belize! This is the Belizean flag," she said, indicating the upper flag. "Below is the Garifuna flag." She stepped over to it and brought her hands across the broad stripes.

"The top stripe, the yellow, is for our Amerindian heritage, for hope and liberation. The white, the middle stripe, is for peace and freedom, which is what we've always sought. The bottom stripe, the black one, it is for Africa, for death and the suffering we have endured." She stepped away from the flag and smiled. "Now I will tell you of all our fresh fish, and later, I will sing to you. I will sing the national anthem, but first, I must tell you about our wonderful side dishes, and then I will tell you about the fish. My sister, she has made a beautiful potato salad."

Mark laughed. He hoped she would sing before they were done, because it never ceased to entertain him. By now, he knew the words and thought he might just have to sing along. When he got home—back to Ohio—he'd teach the words to his girls, and when he brought them here, one day soon, they could sing it for Cordelia. His daughters could sing, like he could. They did not, thank God, take after Cathy, who sang like a frog.

A small boy came running into the restaurant, slamming the screen door behind him. He stopped suddenly and smiled shyly at the Americans. He was barefoot, wearing an old T-shirt that was too large, covering his knees and most of his calves. He shuffled up to the table and crawled onto Melvin's lap.

"What you got on there, boy?" Melvin asked.

"Your shirt!" He smiled a gap-toothed grin. And they all laughed.

"Wilson? Right?" asked Mark. The boy nodded solemnly and leaned into his father. "I've got a little girl just about your age. Are you five?"

"Seven."

Mark nodded in thought. "Wow! Seven." He was so little to be seven. Mark watched as Melvin rested his hand on the boy's head and kissed him absently on the forehead as he reached for his beer.

"I was thinking," Aaron said, "that maybe we could do a little something for Charlie. Maybe tomorrow? Or Friday. We could wait until Friday, but I don't know when his daughters are leaving. Soon, I think. What do you think? Tomorrow? Maybe take the boats out. Say something? Throw a few Belikins in the water? Eat some food. I think Kendal would be up for it. She's better. She's up. I made her eggs. She didn't eat a lot, but she told me they were good. What do you think? Tomorrow?"

"So, you don't have to kill her father?" Mark asked.

"Well, no. Not yet." Aaron smiled sheepishly. "You know, I will if I need to. But I think they're starting to get it." He took a bite of his rice and beans. "So, what do you think? We could have a Dugu of sorts. Is that what it's called, Melvin?" asked Aaron.

"Well, yes, Dugu. But I don't think that's what you mean."

"Dugu?" Mark asked.

"Feasting of the Dead," said Melvin. "To please the departed soul. But it's always done at least a year after the death. After the spirit has made it known that it's unhappy. The Buyei—the high priest—is there, and he leads the sacred dance to calm the restless spirits. But I think maybe a Beluria is more what you're after, Aaron."

"Beluria?"

"Yes. It's more like one big, long wake—nine days. On the ninth day after the burial, there's a huge-ass party—a burial feast."

"There's no body to bury," said Mark.

"Then nine days from the death?"

"Nine days," said Aaron. "That would be Sunday."

Melvin nodded in thought. "Well, Sunday, then. It's better. Time to gather and prepare. I will talk to the women."

Aaron sat back and smiled. "I'll talk to the daughters."

"And the parents?" asked Mark.

Aaron grimaced. "Maybe someone else should talk to them."

Theresa wasn't so sure about a Beluria. After all, Charlie wasn't a Garifuna; and really, there should be an official start of the nine days, which was generally on a Friday. But when Melvin explained that it wasn't really a Beluria, that it was really more of a wake or a memorial service, then her concerns lessened. "It will be an American version," he said.

"Yeah," said Mark, who'd tagged along, just in case. "Food, drink, saying goodbye, that sort of thing."

They were in Theresa's little concrete home. A curtain separated the living space from the bedroom. The TV was on, and several small children lazed about on the floor. "So a party? A celebration of his life?" she asked.

"A big-ass party," answered Melvin solemnly. "For a good man."

"Yes." Theresa nodded. One of her children, or maybe a grandchild, climbed up into her lap and nestled his head into her bosom. Her arms encircled the child. "He was a good man."

Author Note: Most of the people who have read this story told me they like Charlie the most of all the characters. What's interesting to me as a writer is that when I started writing this story, Charlie didn't even exist, yet he went on to become a pivotal character. It was much the same when I started Legend of the Lost Ass. *I had no intention of telling two stories, seventy years apart, but when I started to write about Ernesto and how he wanted his beloved tractor, Miss Mango, driven to Belize on her own power, I fell in love with the old guy and really wanted to know his story. He went on to become the main character. Writing is so cool that way, how one character can dictate the story arc!*

Chapter 33: Sometimes All You Need Is Laughter

The preparations began almost immediately. Aaron and Melvin organized the building of a temporary structure in front of Kendal's home, made of poles stuck into the sand and palm fronds laid together in a simple weave. The women began to prepare the food, digging up extra potatoes, telling the young men to cut extra plantains from the trees, preparing the coconuts, soaking the beans. A young pig was fed a little extra. Chickens were caught and held in pens so as to hasten the preparation on Sunday. Noel fished a little longer. The daughters agreed to stay. The parents offered money to pay for the food—which was accepted in the form of a donation to the local school. Mark offered to provide the beer and the coconut rum. Kendal sat in her house, in Charlie's old chair, and watched the sea.

They took the boats out late Sunday afternoon, in a soft chop, before the sun was too low in the sky. It was just three boats, with some of Charlie's closest friends, that formed a little circle in the sea. There were a few stray boats in the periphery, there more out of curiosity than function.

Noel stood up in the bow of his boat, and his body swayed with the sea. He twisted the Belikin open. He raised the bottle to the air and said, "To my friend. To rummy. We gave each other crap." He let go of the bottle, and it dropped into the sea.

Frank stood up and uncapped his beer. "To one lucky son of a bitch," he said and let the bottle drop.

"To fishing," said Clement.

"To Charlie," said another.

"May you drink it well," said someone else.

When it seemed to be Mark's turn, he stood up and almost fell as he twisted off the cap. He spread his legs further apart and let his body move with the boat. "Thanks for that tarpin," he said, bringing his hand over the side of the boat.

"Tarpon," corrected Aaron. The other men laughed.

Mark shrugged. "Whatever—thanks for my fish story." But before his fingers would release their grip on the bottle, it became necessary to bring the beer to his mouth; and much to the delight of the other men, he took a nice long swig then let the bottle fly. When the men had stopped laughing, all eyes turned to Aaron.

Mark watched Aaron stand up and open the beer. What was Aaron going to say? What could he say? *Thanks for sharing? Sorry?* Once he started talking, would he ever stop? Would they be out here rocking on this boat forever?

Aaron looked at the beer, looked out to sea. He looked at the men then back to the sea. His eyes closed in pain, and he brought the beer, with two hands, to his chest, where it lingered a moment. With his eyes still closed, he moved the bottle to his lips, kissed it gently, and dropped it into the sea.

Then the party really began. On the beach, there were card games and dominos and punta dancing and drummers and singers and food and a lot of drinking and a lot of weed. There were those who'd wandered in for the party who were no more to Charlie than a slight tip of their chin as they passed on the road. There were children and teenagers, curious tourists, expats, and natives. When it grew dark, a fire was lit. More music was played. Torches were lit. More alcohol was consumed. A young man from the US, a joint hanging from his mouth, who didn't know Charlie from Adam, sat on the overturned kayak, strumming his guitar and crooning Grateful Dead songs. More food was put out. The evening eased into night. Very small children fell asleep against their mothers' breasts. Dogs sat with mournful eyes, their tails gently swaying, hoping beyond hope that the food table would collapse, while ghost crabs, confused by the continuation of the day, scuttled in and out of their holes with frenzied little movements.

She watched from the veranda, her mother sitting near and watching with her, her father lost somewhere in the activities. Someone had brought her a plate of food, which had spent the late afternoon alive with buzzing flies—a dark cloud dancing on the untouched food. She'd watched for hours. Now even the flies had given up and gone to wherever it is that flies go when they sleep. Her mother moved quietly and threw the food away. Her father checked in, calling her Elizabeth, slurring mildly, and then rejoined the activities. Kendal stood up as the moon shifted in the sky and left without a word. Her mother turned her way, followed with her eyes, watched her as she made her way into the house, into the bedroom.

Kendal looked around the dim room, lit only by the lamp on the nightstand. She looked at the unmade bed, the open closet door, Charlie's hats and a couple dirty shirts hanging from its pegs. There was a paperback on his bedside table, open and facedown, his reading glasses nearby. The T-shirt she'd worn yesterday was on the floor; one of her sandals lay by her side of the bed, the other one nowhere in sight. There was the stain on the small braided rug—Charlie's coffee cup had slipped from his hand, just the week before last, the coffee splashing onto the rug, the cup shattering across the tiled floor into too many pieces to fix. Her eyes went to and stayed on the painting above their bed. It was a rather poor rendition of a palm tree and the sunrise, thick with opaque oils. Charlie's one and only attempt at anything artistic. It made her smile.

She stepped from the bed and into their closet, where she ran her hands, her arms, her face through its contents.

Mark tipped back the Belikin and then had to spit it out as laughter exploded from him. "I don't believe it! He really said that?" he said, wiping at his mouth with the side of his arm and falling deeper into the sand.

"Believe whatever the fuck you want." Aaron passed the joint his way. "But that's exactly what Charlie said: 'Take your fucking flounder and stick it up your ass!'"

Mark had to laugh all over again and couldn't quite make connections with the joint. Aaron scooted further into the sand. He was almost touching Mark as they lay side by side, both of them having lost the battle with gravity—the joint glowing somewhere above, against a moonlit sky. The beach was aglow with torch lights and the fire and the big-eyed moon, so that it was almost as light as day. People were strolling about somewhere above their heads, and the drummers were reaching a frenzied pitch, and the palm tree fronds waved against the moon.

"What the fuck?" said Aaron, looking toward the sky.

Mark looked up just as a shirt fluttered to the sand, coming within inches of his face. A young Garifuna man came close and snatched it away. Their eyes shifted to the veranda, and Kendal was there, leaning over the railing, her face a pink glow in the firelight. Her arms came out and up toward the sky. A shirt exploded from her hands and then bloomed outward and floated to the sand.

"From Charlie!" she yelled and threw a pair of trousers. "To Hopkins!" She reached down and then threw a loafer. "He'll be everywhere! Everywhere I look!" Mark had to duck as a sandal sailed past his head.

Kendal's mother was close, wringing her hands. Small children gathered near the veranda, their hands outstretched to the sky.

"For you?" Kendal cried to the children. She tilted her head down their way. "What do I have for you?" She disappeared from view for a long moment and then reappeared, raising her hands into the air and letting go a handful of plastic poker chips, which quivered quickly to the earth. The children screeched with delight as Kendal threw handful after handful of chips then banded decks of cards, a few dice, an old puzzle or two, a half dozen baseball caps. Then she went back to the clothes—shoes raining down, tube socks floating through the air, boxer shorts of various colors—crazy fluttering butterflies...

"Stop it!" cried Julie as she ran across the sand. She stopped below the veranda. "Those are my father's things!"

Kendal paused midthrow and cranked her head to the side. "Did you want them? Did you want them for yourself?" She threw back her head and laughed then let the pants soar.

Aaron began to laugh. He pressed the joint into Mark's fingers and rolled onto his stomach, his head against his crossed arms, and laughed into the sand—the pressure of his merriment too much to bear. Mark's attention was drawn away from Kendal, away from Aaron, and to the small scuffle that had erupted nearby.

"Give me the shoe!" the tall, skinny boy yelled. He was holding a brown loafer in one hand and wrestling a kid about the same age with his other. The shorter, rounder kid held the shoe's partner tight and close to his chest.

"No fucking way!" The tussle deteriorated into the sand. Arms and feet, elbows and knees—sand flying everywhere. A shoe flew loose. Noel was suddenly there, lifting the boys by their arms and shaking the two of them until the other shoe fell free. A smaller, younger boy scurried into the mix, grabbed the pair of shoes, and danced away. Mark's head fell into the sand, and he laughed along with Aaron—a laughter so deep, so pure, that it hurt.

Mark woke up with his face pressed into the sand for what he knew would be the last time. He struggled upward and carefully removed the grains of sand from his ear canal. Aaron was still near, sleeping, one side of his face to the sand, his hair falling across the other side, waves of palm shadows caressing his sun-drenched back. Mark fought the urge to place his hand on this man's shoulder and give it a little squeeze. He would miss Aaron—that was for damn sure.

There were others with them on the beach: prone bodies here and there—some people walking or talking quietly amongst the innumerable empty Belikin bottles, trash, dogs, unclaimed tube socks, and boxer shorts sprinkled about. He would help, later, to clean away the debris. But now, he struggled to his feet and walked the distance to his little home on the beach and made himself a large pot of coffee. He bought a beautiful round loaf of coconut bread from a little girl named Tana and sat on the beach, with his coffee and his loaf of bread, and said goodbye to the morning and hello to the afternoon.

Kendal woke up in her bed and was slapped by the same sadness that had slapped her each time she'd opened her eyes from sleep in the last ten days. But rather than ease back down into slumber or wait until the sorrow poured over her like heavy cream, she rose from the bed, visited the bathroom, and draped on whatever was near. She stepped from the bedroom and took the coffee from her mother's outstretched hand, the small slice of toast with mango jelly, and continued across the room. She had to place the coffee on the floor momentarily to free a hand to turn the handle of her studio door; and as she slipped into the room and reached down to retrieve the coffee, her eyes met those of her mother. She rewarded her mother's worried face with the slightest of smiles before she shut the door, where she reentered and then was lost in her world.

Author Note: I loved writing this memorial party scene. There's nothing like a good party! My favorite part was when the boys fight over Charlie's loafers. I wonder what your favorite part was.

Chapter 34: Just a Melon-Sized Slice out of Time

As the three of them made their way north along the quiet street of the village, Kendal threaded her arm through Mark's and leaned into his body. The day was cast in a light-gray layer of clouds. It was early and the sort of day where anything was possible—rain, sunshine, a quick, violent storm, the continuation of indecision. This was the first time in the twelve days since Charlie's death, to Mark's knowledge, that Kendal had strayed from her home, from her beachfront. She was thin. Dark circles still encircled her eyes, but her face was calm, serene.

Mark and Aaron had wandered down the beach before the sun had barely lit the sky and found her sitting near the shore, wrapped in an oversized shirt and waiting for an unseen sun. They'd asked her to join them for breakfast, and she'd said yes.

As they walked, Mark took in the village, decked out in Christmas finery. Plastic garlands hung from the fronts of restaurants; a large blow-up Santa smiled and waved and rocked in the soft Caribbean breeze; multicolored lights were strung across the road; up near the crossroads, an impressive artificial Christmas tree towered. Iris had sprayed fake snow on the windows of her restaurant and hung a plastic ball of mistletoe above her threshold.

"I'm sorry," Kendal said, pressing her body tighter into his and drawing Mark's attention away from the decorations. "I've failed you."

He stopped and turned to her, saw the mischief in her eyes.

"I never did get you laid." She shook her head sadly.

"Yeah." He smiled. "I was really counting on you. God knows I'm certainly unable to secure a good lay on my own."

"Even a bad one, apparently," offered Aaron.

"Not even a fish," mused Mark.

"Or a chicken!" And Kendal laughed.

"Hey, I have my standards." He tugged gently on one of her dreads. "I draw the line at chickens."

Kendal's other arm found Aaron's, and the three of them, laced together, continued up the road. The village was beginning to come alive. Babies were crying, and the high-pitched voices of small children could be heard through the wooden louvers on the windows of the homes. A mother hen, followed closely by the five tiny puffs of her children, scurried past. A man Mark didn't know carefully wound multicolored Christmas lights around a palm tree. Lara appeared at the doorway of her little block house and shook out a rug above her ever-growing belly. She smiled as they came near. Half a dozen green parrots chattered noisily as they winged quickly overhead. Mark looked up and watched as they disappeared into a clump of trees. One of the village dogs approached, his head down, his tail wagging. A small boy stood naked in his yard. He held his tiny penis in his hand, and as he peed into the sand, he raised his other hand and waved and grinned.

"Good morning!" Kendal called to the boy and laughed as she pulled an arm free to ruffle the dog's head.

As they reached the center of town, Frank stepped from the back of Kassava's and rubbed his hand through his hair and squinted up to the hazy sky.

"Good morning, Frank," Kendal called.

His eyes turned from the sky to her, and his face bloomed into a smile. "I'll have a cold one waiting for you next Friday," he said, pointing at her good-naturedly.

"I'll be there!" Kendal called as they turned to enter the coffee shop that had recently opened.

The place was small, painted bright yellow, with local artists' paintings and carvings decorating the walls, along with the cutout snowflakes and shiny glass ornaments hanging from the ceiling. There were only a couple tables and a little sitting area, which consisted of a handmade padded couch of bent wood and matching chairs, where one could hang out, sipping coffee and perusing the *Belize Times*. Except for the tropical influence, it could have been any cute coffee shop on the streets of Columbus, Ohio.

They were greeted by Dagmar, the owner and an expat from Germany. She and her husband had opened the shop in the late fall, and the place was a welcomed addition to Hopkins. "Hello, Aaron. Kendal," Dagmar said, wiping her hands on a towel and coming from around the counter. She hugged Kendal. "How are you? No. Don't even answer that. You're good, I can tell." She turned her attention to Mark. "Mark. Right?"

"That's right." Mark smiled.

They sat at one of the small tables, and Mark checked his watch. It was almost eight on Wednesday, December 23. He needed to get to Belize City for his one o'clock flight. Aaron had offered to drive him to Dangriga to catch the hopper.

"Coffee? All around?" asked Dagmar. Her husband, Pacin, turned on the music, and gentle Caribbean tunes filled the air.

"Yes, please. And breakfast," Aaron said. "What're you offering today?"

They placed their orders for breakfast burritos. Pacin brought the coffees before returning behind the counter to start on their food.

Dagmar, Aaron, and Kendal gossiped mildly while Mark sipped his coffee and took it all in. He was facing the door and looking into the street, and it wasn't long before the children started making their way up the street for their last day of school before the Christmas break. They were skipping and animated, excited about the holiday, leaning on one another in early-morning laughter. Then a Rasta man, his dreadlocks pulled up into a brightly knit cap, pedaled by on a bike as if moving to the beat of the music; a dog trotted past with definite purpose; there was a farmer sporting a large machete; another group of laughing children; two round women, their hair covered by bright hats, their bodies draped in faded floral skirts; and Mark smiled and sighed and felt warm and sad and prematurely nostalgic.

He rechecked his watch and sighed again.

"We're good," Aaron assured him.

Other people came in, and Dagmar drifted off to take their orders, and Aaron began to talk.

"So, I was surveying the yard yesterday, you know, checking out the grounds. The banana trees we planted, Mark, they're starting to grow! Tiny little green points shooting right out of the sand. A little over eight months and counting. The avocado tree I bought is looking great. Do you know you can start them from the seed, but then they almost never produce fruit? What's the point of that? I guess people plant things just to look at them, but I like to get something from it, you know? They graft them. The avocado trees. I wonder how they do that. And my papaya plant is like some sort of fucking mutant weed."

Kendal grinned. She caught Mark's eye over the rim of her coffee mug as she took a sip, and then they both laughed.

"I guess they don't grow stuff like that in Ohio, do they, Mark?" Aaron asked and actually waited for an answer.

Mark put down his coffee cup and said, "Buckeyes. We grow buckeyes."

"What the fuck is a buckeye?" asked Aaron.

"A nut. A poisonous, inedible nut."

"What's the point of that?"

Mark shrugged as their breakfasts were delivered to their table. "To wear around your neck at Ohio State football games."

"You Americans are fucking weird."

Mark took a bite of his burrito. It was fat and hot and dribbled good stuff down his chin.

"I have something for you," said Kendal.

Mark put his sandwich back on his plate and wiped at his chin with his napkin. He watched as she bent over and fished through her knapsack.

"Somewhere," she muttered.

"So, I was thinking about oranges, you know?" said Aaron. "But I don't think they'll do very good this close to the sea. In fact, I'm a little worried about my avocado. I might just have to buy myself a little piece of land inland. What do you think? I have some money saved. Start a little farm. Build myself a little house."

Kendal's head popped back up. "Here we go." She placed two small, colorful boxes on the table. One was bright red with green dots and the other green with red dots. "For your girls. Something I thought they might like." She placed her hand on Aaron's arm. "You'd be an awesome farmer."

"You think?" Aaron smiled. "Of course, I'd still dive. I'll always dive. Grow just enough for me and some of my friends."

Kendal turned her attention back to Mark. "Open them," she urged.

Mark looked at the boxes and smiled. He'd bought a couple of handmade dolls and a couple of wooden carvings of sea creatures, but that was all he had for his girls. He'd purchased some small gifts for the rest of his family—a beautifully painted clay vase for his mother, handmade Maya earrings for his sister and sister-in-law, carved smoking pipes for his father and brother-in-law, a cool pocketknife with a carved wooden handle for his brother, little carvings and inexpensive jewelry for his nieces and nephews. He'd agonized, but in the end, he'd bought nothing for Cathy.

He wiped his hands more thoroughly and lifted the lids. Mark looked at the silver hearts attached to shiny silver chains nestled in their silken cradles. They were about half an inch in size, lacy, and delicate, with a beautiful mosaic of inlayed stone, each unique and personal in design. Closer inspection revealed the tiny letters of his daughters' names worked magically into the design. He didn't know what to say. He'd seen her jewelry at the resorts, knew her stuff sold for hundreds of dollars. Mark looked up, his mouth in a soft *O*.

She was looking at him, her bottom lip held gently in her teeth. She glanced back at the necklaces and frowned. "I know your girls are young. Maybe this isn't such a good gift."

He brought his hands to hers, bending her smooth, cool fingers within his. "Kendal, thank you. They're perfect. They're beautiful. My girls will love them."

Her eyes met his with a smile.

"Thank you," he said as he reached down and kissed her hand theatrically. "You know... for everything."

Author Note: Even though Kendal may have failed Mark regarding getting laid, I believe she and Aaron (and Charlie) made a world of difference in getting him through the early stages of mourning over his wife's betrayal. I have high hopes for all three of them!

Chapter 35: Later, Moron

It was just a tiny speck in the sky, and as it grew closer, it didn't get big enough. "What the hell is that?" asked Mark.

"It's your plane, you moron."

"That's not a plane. It's a VW Bug with wings—and don't call me moron, asshole."

Aaron laughed as the plane made a noisy landing, turned around, and taxied back toward them. "Seriously. Is that my plane?" Mark asked, and Aaron continued to laugh. He took out his packet of cigarettes and tapped it on his thigh until one eased away from the others.

It was just the two of them. Kendal stayed behind, not particularly wishing to make the trip into Dangriga. Mark had given her a good long hug as they'd left the coffee shop; and then he'd watched, along with Aaron, as she grew smaller and smaller as she headed away toward her home.

Somewhere on the way to Dangriga, a decision had been made by the weather god and the clouds had blown apart, so that now the sky was light blue with puffy white clouds and streams of sunshine creeping through. The sunlight glared off the wings, and Mark brought his hand up to protect his eyes. The plane stopped a short distance from where they were standing and shut off its engines. It was hot and steamy. Waves of heat were pulsing off the asphalt, and they enveloped the plane.

"Really? That's my plane?"

Aaron laughed again. "It's a fifteen-, twenty-minute flight."

"And that makes it better because...?"

Before Mark had a chance to get himself into a total panic, the man from Tropic Air was grabbing his luggage and putting it aboard this impossibly small aircraft.

"My God. You're not kidding, are you?" He looked at Aaron with uncertainty, and Aaron just grinned and lit his cigarette with a long, slow drag.

The Tropic Air man indicated with a slight wave and a smile that Mark could board.

Mark turned to Aaron. "Boy, they don't waste much time, do they? You don't think the pilot needs a little rest, needs to take a leak or something?"

Again, the man waved at him to board.

Mark let out a sigh of resignation. "Well, I guess this is goodbye." He grasped Aaron's hand and gave it a firm squeeze.

Aaron pulled him in for a tight hug, and Mark brought his arms across Aaron's back and breathed in Belize—sweat and salt, coconuts and cigarettes, the sweet smell of weed, a wonderful whiff of Belikin beer.

"Later, moron," Aaron said as he released him.

"Count on it, asshole," Mark replied.

Then he was strolling toward death. He carefully avoided the slowly rotating blades of the prop and crawled aboard. The pilot turned from his seat, gave Mark a little nod, and turned back to the task at hand. It was just Mark and the pilot. The pilot pushed and pulled a few things, and the plane fired back into life. Mark said a few Hail Marys, which weren't going to get him anywhere since he wasn't Catholic and wasn't all that sure there even was a god. But at this moment, as he reached for his seat belt, he hoped to hell there was. He buckled the metal clasp of the seat belt, as if that little strap of cloth was going to make a difference, clutched the armrest with one hand, and waved a final goodbye to Aaron.

Then they were taxiing away, the plane rumbling and grinding a noisy complaint. As they picked up speed, the entire contraption shook until Mark's teeth banged in his head. Mark's hands ached as they dug into the armrests. He watched the oncoming stand of palm trees grow closer and forced his eyes to stay open, the sound of the engines reaching a frenzied roar. Finally, the plane was lifting up, clearing the palms by what looked like inches, and then they were climbing into the sky. Mark closed his eyes, not relaxing the grip on his chair, and sighed. After a minute, when the plane had leveled out, he opened his eyes and looked out the little window. The plane followed the beautiful Belizean coast north, the shadow of the craft following them across the sea. Another soft sigh slipped from his lips. There wasn't going to be much of a chance for onboard cocktail service on this flight. And maybe that was a good thing, Mark thought, as he began the first leg of his long journey home.

Author Note: What do you think? Will Mark return with his girls some day? I don't hold out much hope for his marriage, but I do think he will continue being a great dad—assuming, of course, he survives the plane ride!

Chapter 36: Into the Vast Clear Blue

The weight was almost more than she could bear, more than she remembered, as if the density of matter had somehow increased. The air was hot and oppressive with moisture, as if she were already wet. The sun's rays were intimidating, burning her skin even through her clothing. There was hardly a breeze, but she still rocked uncomfortably, her stomach feeling it and the backs of her thighs pressing too hard against the edge of the boat. Her mouth was already parched from the dry air she was breathing through the mouthpiece. She felt weighed down and burdened. And she felt frightened. It had been so long.

She took in a deep breath and closed her eyes. As she leaned back, giving her body up to gravity, her heart beat hard against her ribcage. She was falling fast, the weight of her burden flinging her toward her destination. It was terrifying and exhilarating—the flash of the clear blue sky, the millisecond of seeing Aaron above her, the even faster glimpse of the uneven line where the sea met the sky. She was bathed abruptly with the cool wetness of the Caribbean, the pressure of the water sucking around her. She sank quickly under the surface, only to pop back into the sunshine like a bobber. She removed one hand from her mask, one from her regulator, and once again found Aaron's face bouncing on the boat. He raised his thumb in a question, and she tapped the top of her head with her hand in answer.

She saw his lips up in a smile before he, too, was falling backward toward the water. His feet flipped into the air, and his body made an impressive splash. He was close now, only inches away from her. He reached out and pulled on her shoulder strap, adjusting some unseen imperfection. His hands rested on her shoulders. They bobbed momentarily, together on the surface, his eyes never leaving hers. The waves splashed against her face, threatening to dislodge her mask. The BCD pushed up against her neck and dug into her armpits.

She was tempted to grab on to him and wrap her legs around his exquisite body, where they could float as one into an unforeseeable future, but Aaron pushed away slightly and gave her a thumbs-down with a smile. She raised her hand in relief, the deflation device over her head, and pressed the button. She sank slowly, beautiful bubbles wiggling around her, the pleasant hiss of escaping air, the welcome watery silence easing away her discomfort.

Kendal was unburdened, floating weightlessly; the only noise was the calmness of her own slow and steady breath. She began to kick her feet, moving horizontally, heading toward a clump of coral straight ahead, huge fans of green and blue coral waving hello, bright colors of fish darting against the blue, the shadow of a small school of blue tang wiggling across the ocean floor, a large grouper watching their approach with lazy caution.

She was almost to the coral when she turned, flipping her body over so that she swam on her back, and found him. He was right there, his eyes smiling beneath his mask, his hair flowing in silken golden strands. He tugged playfully on her flipper. She smiled, her lips moving up around her mouthpiece, her teeth clamping down on the soft plastic. As she blew out the water that had collected in her mouth along with a mass of bubbles, Aaron's face was lost. She kicked her foot free of his grasp, and in one sweeping motion, she flipped and rolled her body forward toward the vast, clear blue of endless possibilities.

Author Note: I hope you enjoyed this story and getting to know Belize and its people. I also hope you enjoy my writing and follow me as an author.

Check out my novel Legend of the Lost Ass *if you'd like to learn a little more about the Maya culture. Thanks for reading!*

Acknowledgments

First and foremost, I want to thank my husband, Paul, whose appetite for adventure has made all our Belizean escapades possible.

I'd also like to thank the members of the CNY Creative Writers Café for their patience with the early drafts of this story.

Special thanks to friend and fellow Red Adept author Shawne Steiger for being instrumental in keeping me writing. Same goes for my darling friend Lorna Lynch.

Last but not least, I want to thank Lynn McNamee, Kim, Liby, and the entire staff of Red Adept Publishing for having faith in this manuscript and allowing it to shine.

About the Author

Karen Winters Schwartz was born and raised in Ohio. She wrote her first truly good story at age seven. Her second-grade teacher, Mrs. Schneider, publicly and falsely accused her of plagiarism. Karen did not write again for forty years.

As a writer and a mental health advocate, she is a sought-after speaker at events and conferences across the country. Karen and her husband moved to the Central New York Finger Lakes region, where they raised two daughters and shared a career in optometry. She now splits her time between Central New York, a small village in Belize, and traveling the earth in search of the many creatures with whom she has the honor of sharing this world.

Read more at www.karenwintersschwartz.com.

About the Publisher

Dear Reader,

We hope you enjoyed this book. Please consider leaving a review on your favorite book site.

Visit https://RedAdeptPublishing.com to see our entire catalogue.

Check out our app for short stories, articles, and interviews. You'll also be notified of future releases and special sales.